Troubles Over The Bridge

A note on the author

Jimmy Ellis went from a working class background to become one of the most famous actors in Britain in the 1960s. As the face of hit police television show *Z Cars*, his performances were seen by up to 19 million people every week in Britain in over 803 episodes across 12 series. He then went onto starring roles in much-loved British television series such as *Playing the Field*, *Ballykissangel* and *One by One* as well as lead roles in the National Theatre and the Royal Shakespeare Company.

However, what many don't realise is that way before his acting roles began, he became artistic director of the Group Theatre in Belfast at the tender age of 27 and fought with writer Sam Thompson to stage a controversial play that dared to tackle the start of the Troubles in Belfast, set in its iconic and famous shipyards. This, more than any of Ellis' acting work, was probably his proudest moment. This book tells that as yet untold tale.

Troubles Over The Bridge

A First Hand Account
of the *Over The Bridge* Controversy
and Its Aftermath

JAMES ELLIS

Lagan Press
2015

www.laganpress.co

Published by
Lagan Press
A Verbal Group Company
Stable Lane, Lane & Mall Wall, Bishop Street Within
Derry-Londonderry BT48 6PU
www.laganpress.co

Cover design by Alex Bones.
Typesetting by Jake Campbell.

ISBN: 978-1-908188-55-7

For my cousin and my oldest friend
Kenneth Jamison

CARPE DIEM

'It doesn't take the time long
Goin' in' – a distinctly Ulster
Turn of phrase; for strangers hard
To grasp – yet you and I, old friend,
Know all too well its implications;
The years have simply flown – 'le temps
S'en va', mon ami – time flies!

Too soon the present fades to memory
As recollections become mere islands
In an infinite sea of vagueness.
Future plans are speculative,
The diary a provisional guide,
Yet the spur of Carpe Diem is still
A powerful drive, so grasp the day!

For when all is said and done, old friend,
It doesn't take the time long...

Goin' in.

James Ellis

Contents

Foreword

For some considerable time I have been thinking about recording my still vivid memories of the controversy surrounding Sam Thompson's first play, *Over The Bridge*, and its eventual staging in the face of a strong and well-orchestrated opposition that continued well beyond the original withdrawal of the play by the board of directors of the Group Theatre. Realising that it is a full half century since this battle of wills took place I feel I must now present my personal version of the story or forever hold my peace. That said, I am aware that in some quarters I may be accused of digging up memories of ...

> old, unhappy, far-off things
> And battles long ago ...

Though in mitigation I might plead that I am not alone in this native tendency, so keenly observed by that witty and wonderful actor, Niall Tóibín:

> "We are now approaching Belfast Airport. Please fasten your seatbelts, extinguish your cigarettes and put your watches back three hundred years."

Unlike the Battle of the Boyne, however, when it comes to *Over The*

11

Bridge, at least I can say I was there, as a 'leading player' and eyewitness, so what follows is my first-hand account.

Because of a determined campaign to deny the citizens of Belfast and beyond the opportunity to judge for themselves what they should see or not see in any theatrical venue in the city, it seemed to Sam and myself that all doors were barred to us. This powerful faction was described at the time by the world famous theatre director Tyrone Guthrie whose advice we had secretly sought, as 'censorship, unofficial, by the establishment' and on account of his wise words we thought it best to tread warily. Because of our initial reticence, in particular with regard to our forming of a production company, wild assumptions were made from the very outset, not only by the press, but by academics and other private individuals involved in the arts, all keen to air their opinions and be seen to be part of the action. Unfortunately, many of these wild assumptions are still taken as gospel truth or a healthy part of the folklore surrounding the drama, while others may be attributed to the charismatic nature of Sam himself who, understandably, grew in confidence and stature as he basked in the unparalleled success and total vindication of his play. He had already hit the headlines by referring to CEMA (the Committee for the Encouragement of Music and the Arts, now the Arts Council of Northern Ireland), as 'The Council for the Encouragement of the Migration of Artists', while in another rather sweeping if eye-catching statement, he called Northern Ireland 'The Siberia of the Arts', ignoring the more than burgeoning talents of such established artists as Basil Blackshaw and T.P. Flanagan.

In contrast to this, Sam Hanna Bell, the radio producer and writer who was Sam Thompson's first mentor and directed his earlier work for the wireless before his first attempt at a stage play, wrote more sensibly and accurately in a book published in the early 1970s called *Theatre in Ulster*:

"Once upon a time, Bernard Shaw wrote to tell Hugh Quinn

that if he had the wit to write a play he had the wit to get it on. Sam Thompson proceeded energetically to prove the wisdom of this conclusion and his play, produced by James Ellis, opened at the Empire Theatre on the 26 January, 1960."

Yet this generalisation is somewhat misleading, even allowing for the fact that by the 1970s the playwright had become something of a celebrity; but in May, 1959, when news of the play's withdrawal from production broke, Sam Thompson was an unknown writer as far as the stage was concerned having thus far only written dramatised features for the local radio under the guidance of his producer Sam Hanna Bell. As for the professional theatre however, Thompson was completely naïve and had it not been for my resignation as artistic director of the Group Theatre and the firm commitment of almost the entire original cast, including the incomparable J.G. Devlin who was to play the leading role, *Over The Bridge*, in my view, would never have seen the light of day, and most certainly not in the city of Belfast.

In this account I have tried to call to mind, as accurately and honestly as I can, my own personal memories of the time and have sought to reveal some hitherto unrecorded events which half a century ago were shared by only a very limited number of people, almost all no longer in the land of the living.

It is true I have assisted some younger writers in their research, largely sticking to recorded archive material and steering them away from what I regard as speculative and inaccurate accounts that have cropped up over the decades, for the story of Sam Thompson's tussle with authority has proved to be an irresistible magnet for responsible and irresponsible commentators alike, who in the course of time are hailed as 'authorities' on the subject.

One exception to criticism among those who have consulted me, and the vast majority who have not, is Maura Megahey, who I thought at the time was doing a thesis for her doctorate but has since produced

13

a remarkable volume entitled *The Reality of his Fictions: The Dramatic Achievement of Sam Thampson*. This book is by far the finest assessment of Sam's achievement as a playwright that I have come across and it pinpoints from largely reliable sources the principal players in the *Over The Bridge* affair and describes fairly accurately its eventual outcome without of course disclosing the behind the scenes plotting which eventually led to the staging of the play – a human drama in itself which, until now, I have largely kept to myself.

In fairness I must mention that one friend and ally, that delightful man, the late Paddy Devlin, was such a supporter of the play and all that it stood for, that he sometimes got carried away. While I was still in Belfast attempting to steady the boat after the failure of *Over The Bridge* in London, he approached me with a script which I still have, that attempted to dramatise my acceptance of Sam's play for production at the Group Theatre and my subsequent confrontation with the chairman of the board of directors. Paddy said he hoped I would play myself in his 'documentary' which also included a portrayal of my father that was very wide of the mark and who he mistakenly called Sam. He had already shown his script to Sam Thompson who had 'agreed to take part if I would'. Well to be truthful, I had no intention of 'playing myself', because Paddy, like Sam, obviously not having been present at the confrontation, had made the whole thing up. He may have consulted Sam for a second hand account of the proceedings but he most certainly had not consulted me. I was, to put it bluntly, very embarrassed by certain passages, especially the reference to my father:

> "Ellis's father regarded his son's connection with the theatre
> as a form of 'cissy' escapism. He couldn't understand why he
> didn't take a job in the Shipyard as a plater like any other
> normal young man."

Nothing could have been further from the truth – my father was intensely proud of the progress I had made and attended the theatre

14

regularly – but being very fond of Paddy I think I prevaricated, knowing full well that his version of events would never be accepted by the BBC. As far as I am aware this particular piece of 'folklore' has never been circulated. I know that Paddy, when chairman of the Arts Theatre, presented a version of *Over The Bridge*, which I did not see, but which I am sure has helped keep the play alive for a public which may have missed it first time round, as have productions by the Lyric Theatre and, more recently, by Martin Lynch.

You may wonder why I have taken so long to 'come out of the closet' as it were. The reasons why are hard to put into words, but after what was a bitter struggle, it transpired that we won a decisive battle by triumphantly staging Sam Thompson's first play but lost the war by failing to mount his second play – *The Evangelist* – before our new-found home in Victoria Square was sold to be knocked down (a deal brokered by our implacable foe and prime mover in the banning of *Over The Bridge*, the chairman of the Group Theatre and principal partner in the largest estate agents in Belfast, a certain Mr Ritchie McKee).

So why have I chosen this particular moment to speak out? Because, I suppose, I believe time to be a great healer and all the people involved have taken on a dreamlike quality or merely seem like puppets in a toy theatre.

One of Ritchie McKee's daughters, some time after her father's death, approached me in a Belfast restaurant and said loyally: 'My father loved the theatre you know'. I think I replied rather clumsily that I did too, but it was just that we loved it in a different way and from vastly different points of view.

That said, I can only in all honesty, faithfully relate what I remember of what were sensational confrontations, unprecedented in the history of the Northern drama, followed by a new found audience, many of them shipyard workers, who had never before set foot in a theatre. These momentous events I feel it is my duty to recall, and the following

15

text is my last word on the subject, though before I begin, I must make one thing clear. Over the years, it has been widely assumed that Sam Thompson was somehow involved in the day to day running of Ulster Bridge Productions and was at the forefront of all negotiations and transactions, particularly to do with his own work. Nothing could be further from the truth! Sam was a director of the company, like Henry Lynch Robinson, and nothing more. As such, however, I kept him informed of every development and consulted him each step of the way. As the resident playwright and of course a major shareholder he was, needless to say, much better off with the new company than he would have been if contracted at ten percent by the Group Theatre. Furthermore, as the author of a banned play which was staged against all the odds, his future fame was assured.

This book will serve, I hope, as a rather belated response to the poet Tom Paulin, who wrote on a postcard dated 19/11/92:

"Dear Jimmy,
I really enjoyed doing the programme with you yesterday –
This is just to say that you **must** publish your account of the
Over The Bridge affair."

Here it is Tom.

Part One
Over The Bridge

Over The Bridge – A Synopsis
by Denis Tuohy

In an office in the Belfast shipyard Rabbie White, a seasoned draughtsman, sings a hymn as he fills in his football coupon. He's joined by shop steward Warren Baxter. They have some trade union problems to discuss. White says hymn singing is "the only time you'll get people together in loving harmony. Then after the Amen they're at each other's bloody throats again."

There's to be an unofficial meeting at lunchtime, arranged by veteran trade unionist Davy Mitchell. Two workers – one Catholic, one Protestant – who have been exchanging sectarian insults, will confront each other and, Mitchell hopes, simmer down.

Ephraim Smart, a young apprentice who fills the men's tea cans, arrives to tell them that the Protestant, Archie Kerr, won't let him fill his can because he fills the can of the Catholic, Peter O'Boyle. "This kind of thing," says White, "is like a disease, it has a nasty habit of spreading."

The lunchtime meeting between Kerr and O'Boyle is acrimonious, each claiming to have been told damaging stories about the other by union members they are not prepared to name. Kerr says he's heard that O'Boyle is not just a republican Catholic but a member of an illegal

21

organisation which O'Boyle bitterly denies. Davy Mitchell loses patience with them and orders them to leave. After they've gone he and the others talk about secret sectarian groups within the union on both sides of the religious fence.

There is another crisis to be dealt with, also fuelled by religion but in a different sense. Billy Morgan, an ex-official of the union has written a letter to the branch secretary saying that he can no longer reconcile his religious beliefs with trade union membership since "trade unions are ungodly assemblies."

That same evening, in the home of Davy Mitchell, his daughter Marian and Rabbie White's wife Martha, who lives next door, hear an explosion which seems to come from the shipyard. Warren Baxter arrives with worrying news. A shipyard worker has been badly injured. At first the explosion was thought to be an accident but someone claimed it was an IRA bomb and the story spread like wildfire. Already there has been trouble. A mob has ordered Catholic workers off two boats and beaten up one who didn't leave quickly enough.

Baxter says Peter O'Boyle has been warned to stay away from work next day but has said he is determined to come in. White says there will be a mob on the move in the morning looking for Catholics.

Next morning Fox, the head foreman, gets a call in his office from the manager in another part of the yard whose Catholic workers haven't turned up. He needs help but Fox can't offer much. He too is short-handed as his own Catholics, with one exception, have stayed away. The exception is Peter O'Boyle.

Davy Mitchell comes to the foreman's office with Archie Kerr who says there's a mob heading for the shop. Davy leaves and brings O'Boyle back to the office for safety.

Fox wants to call the police but the phone is dead. The line has been cut. Davy goes out to talk to the mob leader. He reports back that if O'Boyle walks out through the gate after the lunch break no harm will come to him. O'Boyle says he won't go.

From outside, the mob leader lets it be known that he wants to talk to O'Boyle alone. This is agreed and the others leave the office. The mob leader is calm, cool, sinister. He says he persuaded the others to wait until ten past one. "If you're still here that crowd will smash your skull."

O'Boyle screams at him in rage. Davy Mitchell and the others come back and the mob leader leaves. Since O'Boyle is still determined to go back to work, Davy, despite protests from the others, insists on going with him.

Through the office window Baxter reports on what's happening. The angry shouting has stopped. There's a deadly silence. Then a frenzied attack on the two men.

Later, in the Mitchell family home, we learn that Davy has been killed and Peter O'Boyle is in hospital with serious injuries.

Fox, the head foreman tells Marian that he knows he once regarded her father as a troublemaker but admired his courage in defending a workmate's right to work. Warren Baxter who has been out drinking starts an argument about the union and about a rule book that couldn't deal with bigotry and brutality.

"A man told me yesterday," he says, "that when the mob went into action he walked away, and so did hundreds of his so-called respectable workmates because they said it was none of their business …. and that's what frightens me… they walked away."

Denis Tuohy played Ephraim Smart, the tea boy, in the original production of Over The Bridge *during its Dublin run in February and March 1960.*

For years many people in Northern Ireland had walked away from sectarian bigotry. Some of them, in positions of authority, did their utmost to prevent James Ellis and Sam Thompson from staging *Over The Bridge* – a play that is not shy about confronting sectarianism.

However, when it opened in Belfast, audiences flocked to see it in record-breaking numbers. Among them were hundreds of shipyard workers, few of them regular theatregoers, who came to witness and applaud a compelling portrayal of uncomfortable truths about their place of work.

I

It was a bright March day in 1959 just a few days before my twenty eighth birthday when I was stopped in my tracks by the playwright and former shipyard worker, Sam Thompson. It was on the pavement between the old Group Theatre and the Northern Ireland BBC in Bedford Street and Sam was in no mood to be brushed off.

'You're the new theatre director aren't you?'

'That's right Sam,' I replied.

'Well, I have a play here you won't touch with a bargepole,' he said, brandishing the manuscript under my nose.

'Why don't we go for a pint and you can tell me all about it,' I suggested, 'and I promise I'll read it tonight.'

This was plainly music in Sam's ears. Obviously I was a man after his own heart.

At this point I knew very little about Sam although I had appeared in two of his BBC Radio Documentaries, one of which was *Tommy Baxter Shop Steward* in which I played the part of Baxter but on these occasions his attention was focused on his mentor and producer, Sam Hanna Bell, who, being a distinguished writer himself, had no doubt shaped and edited Sam's work and in all probability written or rewritten parts of the script himself, so our first real meeting was the challenging confrontation on the street followed by our first friendly exchange of our hopes and ambitions in a snug of the old Elbow Room, then just across the road from the BBC and a favourite watering place for their producers and members of the Group Theatre company.

The first impression I formed of him was that of a forthright but not unfriendly man with challenging eyes, a full face and a shock of dark brown hair that partly covered his ears. His shoulders were broad and his body was slightly on the portly side, no doubt because of his fondness for a pint of Guinness; but he could obviously handle himself in a shipyard confrontation. In short, a man's man, like my father.

The first thing we discovered about each other was that we were both from East Belfast, the next, to our amazement and delight, was that we were born within a couple of hundred yards of each other, he in Montrose Street off the Albertbridge Road, and I at number 13 Gawn Street in a house now demolished, off the Newtownards Road. Needless to say, we got on famously on that occasion and established a bond that continued after my departure for London where he stayed in my flat near the BBC's Television Centre. The best characteristic of Sam, however, is, I believe, expressed in his own words to the electors of South Down where he stood against the Conservative/Unionist candidate Lawrence Orr. His message to the good people of South Down was typical of Sam:

"Those of you who have seen my plays, heard my broadcast social documentaries, or read my articles in the press, will know two things about me.

"The first is that I care about people as people; I am angered at the pensions on which old people have to live; I know from my own past experience the misery caused by unemployment and I am bitter that a new generation of young people are suffering it still. Our children have a right to a decent education, a fair opportunity in life and a livelihood without forced emigration.

"The second is that I am a forthright person and I am not afraid to speak up for my sincere opinions. People no longer want words and promises, they want action. If you elect me your member of Parliament, I will speak frankly and act decisively on your behalf – which is more than the weak contingent of unionists have done. If, as I believe, Labour forms the next Government, South Down will need a spokesman on the Labour benches."

Needless to say, his words fell on deaf ears. Over the next couple of years Sam Thompson became a close friend, not only of my late father, but also of the leading actor in his most famous play, the much loved J.G. Devlin.

I read the play that afternoon and took it back to my parents hoping my father, himself a shipyard worker, would cast his eye over the script. Not only did he do that but he sat poring over the entire play, re-reading many passages. When he had finished, at well past midnight, he handed it back and took off his glasses before saying, 'This is our play, son, you must do it.'

Now my father, with little education, was nevertheless a very intelligent man and his judgement was exactly what I wanted to have, especially as he had spent his entire working life in the shipyard. I envisaged shipyard workers queuing at the box office to see 'their play' when word got around,

Perhaps I should explain at this point how a lad from my background became first an actor and then a director. I had attended primary, (then called 'public elementary') schools on the Newtownards Road, in Birkenhead, where my father was forced to go in search of employment, and on the family's return to Belfast, firstly at McClure Street School off the Lower Ormeau Road, then again after war broke out in September 1939, at Strand Public Elementary School in Sydenham where I am proud to say, a commemorative plaque marks my schooldays. My mother's brother, the resourceful Uncle Johnnie, found quite elegant attic houses in a terrace at very cheap controlled rents because of the fear of air-raids due to the proximity of the large shipyard and Short and Harland's aircraft factory. It is there, I think, at 30 Park Avenue, off Connsbrook Avenue, that my story really begins, though that house was to be our family home for the next 60 years until my elder sister, Eileen, was taken into care in the year 2000. It now has a commemorative plaque.

From Strand School to my utter surprise and my parents' delight, I won a City Scholarship – only 200 were awarded at that time, 100 for girls and 100 for boys – and I went to Methody, (the Methodist College), where I received an education which has remained with me for my entire life; I had attained four distinctions and three credits but in a highly competitive coterie of around a dozen of the brightest pupils in a school which housed around 1,400, I had to literally talk my way into the exclusive Upper Sixth Form in an interview with the amiable but exacting vice principal 'Pop' Rose. While at least two thirds of our little group won places at Oxford, Cambridge and Trinity College, Dublin, my close friend James Greene the actor, presenter and announcer for Ulster Television and myself won scholarships to Queen's University, Belfast. Though James finished the course and got his degree, I was a poor student. However, both Jimmy Greene and myself joined the Dramatic Society and as 'freshers' appeared in Shaw's *Candida*.

We both in that same year appeared regularly at Hubert Wilmot's Arts Theatre which was then in Fountain Street, receiving I think around £3 per week, much needed money as neither of our families could afford to support us. Jimmy soldiered on but I fell by the wayside. However, at this opportune moment, I won the prestigious Tyrone Guthrie Scholarship – the only one ever awarded and supported by CEMA – which was a carefully thought out scheme to attend the Bristol Old Vic school, work backstage at every aspect of stage management, attend rehearsals of particular productions, including Hugh Hunt's acclaimed London production of Shakespeare's *Love's Labours Lost* and direct a play of my own choosing using my fellow students, at Bristol University. I chose T.S. Eliot's *The Cocktail Party* with my cast featuring Phyllida Law, the mother-to-be of Emma Thompson who became the first wife of our Kenneth Branagh. At this point I had made a firm decision not to make a mess of this opportunity and do something meaningful with my life. I had caught the acting bug, or would it be a predisposition for directing? Only time would tell. I was in my early twenties and the die was cast.

My first job was arranged by Tyrone Guthrie and directed by Hubert Wilmot. It was a tour of *The Glass Menagerie* by Tennessee Williams that opened at Portstewart and the salary was £11 per week, an unheard of sum for me who had hitherto only earned at most £3 per week. Though I didn't know it at the time, it was in this production that I met my future first wife, Betty Hogg. When I rejoined the Arts Theatre's regular company Mr Wilmot, affectionately known as 'Hibbie', tried to reduce my salary to £2 per week because he said I had forgotten everything he taught me! I was outraged at the remark and immediately approached Harold Goldblatt who was the director of the Ulster Group Theatre. 'Harry' received me warmly and shrewdly asked me what Wilmot had paid me. I mentioned the £11 per week but he countered with 'Ah that was for a tour', so I had to confess that my usual salary or fee was £3 per week quickly adding, 'but that was before my training at the Bristol Old Vic.' The scholarship had been widely publicised.

Mr Goldblatt thought for a moment and then said: 'Well I haven't got a part for you at the moment but I'd like you to join the company which I'm sure you know is far and away above the standard of the Arts Theatre' he added, dismissively. 'I can offer you £3 a week for doing nothing' he said, adding 'You won't have to brush the stage or do any menial backstage tasks; nor will you have to understudy.' Though on the face of it the prospect seemed disappointing, it was an offer I couldn't refuse; and so, in this humble capacity, I joined the prestigious Group Theatre.

So what was the Group like and what were my first impressions? I remember clearly that I was overawed and truly astonished at the standard of the acting in a company I had never seen in action. Outstanding, I would have to say, was R.H. McCandless who could effortlessly evoke throughout an entire performance what has been described as 'the willing suspension of disbelief'. In short, he was a master of his craft. He was closely followed by the inimitable J.G. Devlin, Elizabeth Begley and Margaret D'Arcy who appeared in more upmarket plays such as *The Heiress* with Harold Goldblatt, Denys Hawthorne and an augmented company which were loyally attended by her many fans from the posher areas of Belfast. Younger members of the company including myself were Maurice O'Callaghan, J.J. Murphy, Kathleen Feenan, Catherine Gibson and later Colin Blakely and Doreen Hepburn, who were to make their mark in London. Colin was already a stage star when he died tragically early from leukaemia.

How I ended up as Artistic Director of such a distinguished company while still in my twenties is a long story but I shall be as brief as possible. First let me explain how I first met with a young actor, who, like myself, was at the time surplus to requirements. He was Billy Millar, who was soon to become a film star after changing his name to Stephen Boyd, starring with Charlton Heston in the film *Ben Hur* as a charioteer. He won the coveted Golden Globe Award for that role before going on to appear opposite such famous names as Gina Lollobrigida, Sophia Loren and Brigitte Bardot. He was first choice to star with Elizabeth Taylor as Anthony in *Anthony & Cleopatra* ahead of Richard Burton, but he was so in demand that his Hollywood agent opted for another film about the Roman Empire starring himself and Sophia Loren.

Over a coffee in an old actors' and artists' meeting place – Campbell's Coffee House – Billy told me he was going to try his luck in London. Harold Goldblatt had told him that the next production was to be a play called *Cartney & Keveny* and Harry had suggested that Billy should play the part of Keveny. He hadn't told Harry yet that he was leaving but was sure I would be offered the part. Well I was and it was a disaster. Whereas Billy was rugged, handsome and mature-looking I had none of these qualities and looked as though I was a callow youth still in my teens. All these things I was aware of as I went in, simply terrified, to attend the first rehearsal.

On that first day, to my amazement, I made one firm friend – R.H. McCandless – the most senior member of the company. That friendship became long-standing and continued to the end of his life. He was inimitable and is sadly missed. The director of *Cartney & Keveny* was a fussy, rather pedantic little man who shall remain nameless. He had been a producer at the nearby BBC and directed the occasional play at the Group as well as excelling in usually comic cameos. Well, maybe he disagreed with Mr Goldblatt about my appearing in his cast and I can't say I blame him, but he fiddled, fussed and interrupted me on every line, got down on his knees, appeared between my legs putting my feet together or slightly apart before rising and putting my arms firmly by my side.

Towards the end of the first morning, R.H. had had enough. 'Leave the lad alone,' he stormed. 'Give him a chance to settle down,' and worse was to follow! 'You're trying to get him to play the part the way you did thirty years ago and bloody awful you were too!' Well a furious row broke out between the old boys and people started to leave the rehearsal room. 'Stay where you are,' the director shouted, 'I haven't finished!' 'Well I have,' Mr McCandless shouted back, 'and young Jimmy is coming with me!' And with that he put his arm around my shoulder and led me out on to the street. 'Be back at 2 o'clock sharp,' the angry old director yelled after us as R.H. suggested we go to the Elbow Room, find a quiet snug, have a bowl of stew and a Guinness and talk things over. I don't remember everything about that tête a tête with the great man but I do remember he was kindly and full of words of wisdom. 'I think after my outburst,' he said with a smile and a wink 'he'll give you time to settle down. You know you're miscast I'm sure, but Harry is too mean to engage somebody of the right age so you're stuck with it. As we learn from our mistakes we can also learn from difficult and sometimes impossible hurdles. I think you can make something of this role and I will give you all the help I can but don't try to turn it into a character part. I think it would be a mistake; Keveny has no obvious eccentricities in his make up.' Then he said smiling as he gathered his thoughts, 'Supposing you were playing my brother and your performance was perfect in every way. Let's also suppose that neither the audience nor the critics were aware of your age. You wouldn't be given full credit for your achievement unless you wore a placard around your neck saying in large letters R.H. McCandless is 79 and I am only in my early twenties,' and his clear blue eyes twinkled merrily at his own obvious improvisation. It is a wonderful memory of a great actor and I treasure it still.

When J.G. Devlin, who was the theatre's Equity Deputy (or shop steward), learned that I had been cast in the forthcoming production he made sure that I had a provisional Equity Card and when rehearsals started that I was entitled to full membership due to my appearances at the Arts Theatre. On the first Friday of these rehearsals we went to see Harold Goldblatt at the box office where our pay envelopes were ready. J.G. Devlin was in the office with Harry. When my envelope was handed over, J.G. called out, 'Hang on a minute, open it up.' Then, 'How much is in it? Hand it over.' Having counted it, he called out, 'What's your game, Harry, you know the rules. This isn't the equity minimum. Hand over the rest.' And it was done, not I may add without a deal of moaning and prevaricating. In due course J.G. put me up as deputy to succeed him while he covered a wider field which included the Northern Ireland BBC.

Though my rise to become artistic director of this wonderful company was not exactly meteoric, it was still swift enough and happened as I remember in three stages; but first of all I shall try to recall the more significant parts I played along the way. Although my first part was a disaster, soon afterwards I was fortunate to be directed by my hero R.H. McCandless in a play by Louis Dalton called *They Got What They Wanted* in which R.H. also appeared with the formidable but friendly Elizabeth Begley, herself an exceptional actress. The very talented Kathleen Feenan and myself played the younger parts. I got my first real break appearing with Elizabeth Begley, as her son in the George Shiel's play *The Rugged Path*. I was beginning to be accepted by the company as a younger member who was pulling my weight. I had an enjoyable cameo role in Joseph Tomelty's long running success *Is the Priest at Home?* which went to the old Cork Opera House before it was burnt down. Two more plays I remember were *The Playboy of the Western World* by Synge, in which I played the lead role, and Jimmy Devlin said I was the best playboy he had ever seen, and that included Cyril Cusack – a compliment indeed! The other one was another Shiels play and since J.R. Mageean was unavailable I stood in for him.

Again R.H. McCandless gave me sound advice. 'Don't try to age him,' he said, 'and don't try to copy Mageean. The part of Specky Boyce can be any age. Little round glasses, a battered old hat to come down enough to flatten your ears and cover your hair, which will be presumed to be grey, maybe silver sideburns, a little shadow under the eyes and at the sides of your cheeks, a slightly pink nose, a squeaky voice, a tatty scarf, plus a shabby fawn raincoat which you never take off. All that should do the trick for you, and,' he added with a friendly twinkle, 'your acting will do the rest. You are learning every day.' The play was *McCook's Corner* in which J.G. Devlin played, quite brilliantly, the part of McCook. It was to exchange with the old Abbey Theatre in Dublin, the very building that was the spiritual home of the poet and playwright W.B. Yeats, Lady Gregory, the Fay brothers, Sarah Allgood and other fine actors of that original company. Sadly, like the old Cork Opera House, it was burnt down shortly after our visit. It is a sobering thought that I don't know of any surviving actors who played in that historic theatre except for me.

So what happened next? Well, at the end of these appearances and one or two more that I have forgotten, Marjory Mason, who was running a repertory company in Bangor, approached Harold Goldblatt and asked if he could provide an actor to take on a leading part at very short notice. Marjory had engaged an actor to join the company but he hadn't shown up. Harold, who was always keen to cut costs, approached me and I jumped at the chance. I had three days' rehearsal but I learned the lines and went on stage word perfect. Marjory was delighted and as she stepped forward as leading lady to take her bow, she made a short speech and explained that I had only three days to rehearse the part. She led me forward and to my utter surprise I was given a standing ovation. As I hurried back into the line, Marjory whispered into my ear that they would expect a speech. As the curtain rose and fell again I fled, costume, make-up and all across the road to the Imperial Hotel where the amiable landlady, 'The Widow Morgan', kept a very small bar, reserved for the actors of Marjory's company.

Marjory asked me if I was prepared to remain with her company until the end of the season when she planned to take a break and try her luck in London or the provinces. I agreed on condition she allowed me to direct a play, which she did. The play was *Murder Mistaken*, a thriller by Janet Green. My future wife, Betty Hogg, had joined Marjory's company and she suggested that Councillor Tom Bailey, a former MP and erstwhile Mayor of Bangor, might back us and guarantee us against loss while we formed a company and chose a programme of plays. Meanwhile on Marjory's recommendation Bailey employed Betty as a manager of a hotel he owned at nearby Donaghadee while I picked up work at the BBC.

We now had the nucleus of a company: James Greene, his girlfriend Diana Payan, Betty and myself. Now we had to find a character lady and two men of middle age, one of whom was dashing looking. Artro Morris fulfilled this role and could play cads, seducers or charming young men when required or older parts when necessary. This company was assembled after a one day visit to London to see an agent called Vincent Shaw. We certainly had a character lady but the one I remember best was called Pamela Pitchford who deservedly had some success in the better provincial theatres of England. A designer – Lewis Logan – and a very experienced, retired stage carpenter completed our company and we were ready to go after we had chosen our first half-dozen plays or so.

It was generally agreed that James Greene would be leading man and Betty Hogg would be leading lady and that I would be the producer/director. I relate all this and more to any who would question my ability or experience to direct *Over The Bridge* or pass judgement on Sam's second, unfinished effort, *The Evangelist*. Our season began with *Captain Carvallo* by Denis Cannon described as a 'traditional comedy' and our little theatre was officially opened by the elderly literary figure Lynn Doyle, a distinguished writer of short stories. We set out our plan and formed a Theatre Club organised by Mrs Hanna, a local Bangor lady who also ran our box office. The enterprise was an unqualified success where not only a nucleus of Bangor residents supported us loyally but many people, especially the young to middle-aged drove down from Belfast to see our productions, some to take advantage of a combined deal to have theatre tickets and an early dinner at the Imperial Hotel. Outstanding I think among our productions were Fry's *The Lady's Not for Burning*, Shaw's *You Never Can Tell* and Wilde's *The Importance of Being Ernest*. These last two plays, being packed to the roof, actually ran for two weeks and we were seriously considering turning our little company into a fortnightly rep. We were obviously a serious threat to the Group Theatre which was not attracting new playwrights and the Arts Theatre was not living up to its name by presenting lowbrow comedies without the talent to adequately deliver the goods.

Our end came about in a curious way. The Arts Council's interest had obviously been aroused and I am convinced that its director, John Lewis-Crosby had made one, if not several, visits to our theatre without announcing his presence. Anyway, we were offered an Arts Council (CEMA) tour, and in the meantime Joseph Tomelty, that most lovable of men, asked me if I would direct his latest play, *To Have A Little House*. I was flattered that he had come to me instead of his old Alma Mater, the Group Theatre but I knew he would need all the help and

35

consideration I could give him after the appalling accident which left him in a coma for eleven weeks. I told Tim Artro Morris, who had scene after scene with Joe to learn both parts and be prepared to improvise if Joe got into trouble. We had three weeks' rehearsal but the first night was a disaster. Worse still, it was packed with 'celebrities', journalists who had come over from England and other VIPs among them the playwright and director of the Abbey Theatre, Lennox Robinson who had travelled up from Dublin.

The worst moment occurred because of Joe's brother who had got himself a seat in the front row. Well-meaning but rather the worse for wear, he had come to support Joe and got the impression that it was a comedy. Every time Joe managed to get to the end of a line or a paragraph his brother laughed and applauded. In the end this got to Joe and he took an uncontrollable fit of the giggles, and then announced he was going for a pee. Sensing trouble I dashed from the rear of the auditorium and found Joe leaving by the front door. He had recovered from the giggles and I managed to persuade him to return to the stage. Meanwhile I was told that Artro had improvised brilliantly and that Joe's brother had been removed from the front row and taken across the road for a drink. The play continued to be an utter failure and limped on to dwindling audiences until the end of the week.

Meanwhile we had to prepare for our CEMA tour of my production of the Post-Restoration comedy *The Careless Husband* by Colley Cibber. It may not have been the best choice for some of our venues but many of the towns we visited had thriving dramatic societies and the audiences in general were surprisingly knowledgeable and sophisticated and overall the tour was acknowledged to be a success.

When we got back to base the place was in a shambles. Joe, in a brave but impossible attempt to revive some of the old favourites and re-establish himself as an actor, had unfortunately failed and petrol rationing added to our woes; our supporters from Belfast seemed lost forever and our Bangor audiences had dwindled perhaps feeling let down by our departure. We held a meeting with our generous backer whose investment during our golden days was a sound one. Now we all felt it was time to blow the whistle on our enterprise; and meanwhile Diana had become Mrs Greene and Betty Hogg had become Mrs Ellis.

Betty and myself went to London to try our luck, while Jimmy Greene got a job with Ulster Television where he introduced Laurence Olivier, who was to open the new station. Meanwhile yours truly and Mrs Ellis were not having much success and I was reduced to selling ladies' shoes in Selfridges. Harry Towb got me my first job by ringing me up and telling me he had had to turn down a part on BBC Television because his agent had found him a better one. The kindly supervisor allowed me to have a day off and I was cast in the first episode of a series about famous escapes from Stalag Luft Three, as an Irish pilot who made a daring escape from the notorious prison camp as the accomplice of a more senior American officer. The episode was called 'The Wire Cutters' and it was later made into a film called *The Great Escape* starring Steve McQueen. The only other cause for excitement, and it was the course that I really wanted to follow, was that I was down to a shortlist of two to direct a play at the Arts Theatre, London called *The Cupboard*.

The next development came out of the blue. I received a letter or a phone call from I think it was John Lewis-Crosby offering me the job as Assistant Artistic Director of the now CEMA funded Group Theatre. It was a path I wanted to follow and I accepted with alacrity, though slightly overawed at the prospect of having to direct my heroes, both male and female, including the elder statesmen R.H. McCandless and J.G. Devlin, along with the formidable Elizabeth Begley and Margaret D'Arcy.

At first I had little to do though there already seemed to be a clash of personalities between the chairman, Ritchie McKee and Harold Goldblatt who had been used to running his own show with his own 'elder statesmen'. One crisis arose over Harold's tendency to make promises to aspiring playwrights and then fail to put their plays on. One of these playwrights had taken legal action and others were threatening to follow suit. I remember little of the author or the play except that the leading character was obviously written for Harry. In an effort to dig my boss out of a hole, I said that though it needed a lot of work, it could be a passable vehicle for Mr Goldblatt who, clutching at straws, said that if I thought so much of it, I could direct it. It was to be my first production and there would be little time to meet the author and make the necessary alterations; then, that very evening, Harry rang me and said without giving any reason that he would be unavailable to play the part. I was furious and said that in that case I would not direct it. He backed down.

Anxious to recover from an inauspicious start, I set about adapting J.B. Priestley's Yorkshire comedy *When We Are Married* to a town in County Antrim – obviously Ballymena – and had no trouble getting permission from Priestley's agent. No script was asked for, just the royalties. The Northern Ireland setting was to emphasise even more sharply the polarity and suspicion that exist in England as well as Ireland. By the time the script was ready I had assembled a first rate cast and there were outstanding performances from J.G. Devlin, Harold Goldblatt, John McBride, Elizabeth Begley and I believe, Gertrude Russell and Irene Bingham. The most riveting performance of all, however, came from the inimitable R.H. McCandless as the tipsy photographer whose near flawless instincts I was loath to interfere with. One awkward moment, however, did arise. In my adaptation the photographer made his reappearance after a lengthy visit to the pub when the three couples, staring glumly out front, were sitting on two settees having already found out that instead of celebrating their silver wedding anniversary, they were not married at all. The door opened and R.H. made his appearance when I ventured to interrupt. 'I was just wondering,' I said tentatively, 'if instead of staying upstage at the door …' 'I was intending to move forward a bit and steady myself with one hand on each settee then deliver the next line level with the six glum expressions.' 'But you really won't be able to see their faces from that position,' I said waiting for his reaction, but he politely waited for me to finish, so I said: 'Would you like to try swaying unsteadily downstage and missing the gap between the sofa at the first attempt then taking aim again and managing to end up facing the audience then, steadying yourself again swivel on the spot and deliver the line upstage …' adding feebly that the audience would be able to enjoy the expressions of the three couples changing from glum to self-righteous outrage.

He thought for a moment before saying: 'I have been told that I have an expressive face, expressive hands and even expressive eyes,' he said, 'but never before today has it been suggested that I have an expressive backside!' Incidentally, his next line was, 'Does anybody fancy a nice game of cards?' I muttered lamely that it was a bad idea and that he should do it his own way and this was done throughout the remaining rehearsals.

At the first performance, to my utter amazement, this is what occurred at this moment in the play. The door swung open very slowly apparently untouched by hand and R.H. McCandless appeared in the gap with his right hand limply balanced in mid-air to indicate that it was he who had opened it before placing the palm of this hand on the door jamb. He got a spontaneous round of applause during which he remained perfectly still. He then placed his left palm on the other jamb to steady himself and subtly convey that he had been drinking. It had the desired effect. All the men in the audience whispered to their wives that he was 'full' (drunk) and this produced immediate laughter and another round of applause.

What followed next took me completely by surprise as he set off on an unsteady arc and instead of steadying himself with the ends of the two settees, he missed the gap entirely before taking aim and negotiating it at the second attempt with a swerve and a stagger, then, after arriving downstage facing the audience, he spun perilously on the spot before placing his feet well apart, facing upstage, and leaning back dangerously. Only then, after a lengthy pause, did he deliver the line, 'Does anybody fancy a game of cards?' It literally brought the house down. Such was his genius.

As I went backstage to congratulate the cast, who had all been brilliant, I was apprehensive to say the least, but when I got to R.H. I caught his eye smiling in the mirror as he removed his make-up. He stuck his right hand over his left shoulder and said, 'You were right, son.' It was, and still is one of the proudest moments of my life.

Among other highlights I remember of that apprenticeship as assistant artistic director was a production of *Picnic* by the American playwright, William Inge. Colin Blakely gave a brilliant performance in the leading role with a strong supporting cast including Betty Hogg and Diana Payan, both formerly members of the Bangor Repertory Company. The critic, Tom Carson, singling out Colin Blakely, called it "A picnic and a feast". The setting, by Lewis Logan who went to London and became a designer for a prominent television company before moving to Hollywood as an art director, was outstanding.

The project that most appealed to our chairman, Ritchie McKee, who was a business man, was my carefully drawn up plan to cover the increasingly lean summer months at the Group Theatre by exchanging their known successes with proven favourites of the Bangor audiences which were augmented by holiday makers, as Bangor was at its peak as a resort in those days. This was made possible by enlarging our personnel with financial aid from Bangor Borough Council.

The first three plays of my planned programme will be discussed in due course but one playwright I must mention is the now celebrated Brian Friel. He had submitted what was his first play, *The Francophile*, which was adapted from one of his short stories. It had some of the flaws of inexperience but it had a leading part tailor-made for J.G. Devlin. I had shown it to J.G. who was excited by the role but I had not yet had the privilege of meeting Brian who lived in Derry. Sadly, however, the controversy that was soon to engulf *Over The Bridge* was so all-consuming that I never got the opportunity to stage a play by one of the most outstanding playwrights of my generation, Brian Friel.

To return to that day in 1959 when Sam and I met for the first time. Having secured the seal of approval from my father, which meant so much to me, I immediately decided to put *Over The Bridge* on my press release as the second of the three plays that would mark my debut as the newly appointed artistic director. Sam's ebullient personality was just what a press conference needed to enliven the proceedings and I was sure he would oblige with a histrionic performance. I had not counted on him overdoing it however and drawing the chairman's attention to the controversial nature of his play, but this is exactly what occurred.

At once, the chairman began lobbying to see the script, a move which I strenuously opposed on the grounds that there were already checks and balances in artistic matters, including a reading committee, which had unanimously passed the play for production. Sensing danger I challenged McKee's need rather than his right to read the play and warned the cast not to leave their copies lying around. Furthermore, I told him that only enough scripts had been printed for cast and stage management.

By now, the opening night of my first production, *The Country Boy* by John Murphy was imminent. It proved to be a success, guaranteeing us a run of at least six weeks and leaving adequate rehearsal time for *Over The Bridge*, before which many cuts, rewrites and rearrangements would be made by the author and myself. Sam proved to be the most cooperative of playwrights and as we got down to business, I would pull his leg about how he could write 'another part of the shipyard' as casually as Shakespeare would write 'another part of the forest'. Our designer, Henry Lynch Robinson, a skilled architect, coped with all our changes of direction with consummate skill. Soon we were ready for the first day's rehearsal with a fixed ground plan and a more or less workable script.

The personality and aspirations of our chairman are crucial to an understanding of the unforeseen bombshell that was soon to follow. Mr Ritchie McKee was a well-connected and influential business man who was used to getting his own way. He was a brother of the Lord Mayor of Belfast and managing director of the largest estate agents in the city. In addition to his extensive business and property interests, he was also chairman of The Group Theatre and The Arts Theatre; but perhaps more surprisingly, he was also chairman of CEMA, from which the two theatres received revenue. He held one other significant honorary position, that of regional governor of the Northern Ireland BBC in which capacity he paid frequent visits to London to complain about programmes that he thought reflected badly, so he thought, on the people and politics of the loyal province of Ulster. On such occasions he was invariably accompanied by Mr 'Harry' McMullan, Head of Programmes, BBC Northern Ireland, who just happened to be our vice chairman. These two appointments were ostensibly to keep an eye on expenditure and running costs but their roles proved in the end to be more far-reaching.

Ritchie McKee had friends in high places and betrayed all the instincts of a natural courtier, being seen in all the right places, especially on formal occasions and in formal dress. He was a friend and golfing partner of Viscount Brookeborough, the Unionist prime minister of Northern Ireland and was often seen in his company, so it is a natural assumption that anything vaguely subversive was reported back to the very highest authority. It was now becoming clear that Ritchie suspected Sam's play of being subversive.

On the first afternoon of rehearsal after an uneventful run through and the first moves to set the action in motion, Mrs Andrews, Ritchie McKee's indomitable secretary entered the rehearsal room: 'The

Chairman wants to read the script,' she announced imperiously, her glance taking in every corner of the room. Only then did I notice she was accompanied by one of the box office girls. The silence was broken when I heard myself offering the same excuse as I had given earlier: 'There are only enough scripts to go round the cast.' By now Mrs Andrews had left the room in a huff and the box office girl had disappeared with her. Only towards the end of the afternoon did a member of the stage management notice that her copy of the play had gone missing. Now the fat was in the fire and we could only speculate as to what the consequences might be. Speculation continued in the actors' favourite bar, the famous Elbow Room, but after a couple of drinks everyone went home looking forward to the next day's rehearsal. What a difference a day makes! When we got to the rehearsal room (a large warehouse in Bedford Street) Mrs Andrews had already arrived. She waited her moment before asking, 'Is everyone present?' The answer being in the affirmative she continued: 'Rehearsals are cancelled. The chairman has called an emergency meeting and Mr Ellis and Mr O'Callaghan are required to attend. The cast will be informed of the outcome.' It was a bolt from the blue. I told the members of the company to assemble in The Elbow Room and that we would inform them of the outcome.

Maurice O'Callaghan was one of the two actors' representatives on the board and also was to play the part of Peter O'Boyle, a leading character in the story. He was also a member of the reading committee which had passed the play for production. We said little as we walked the short distance from the warehouse to the theatre and the board room and I remember little of my feelings at the time except perhaps for a certain numbness. As we entered the room the comic nature of the confrontation remains uppermost in my mind. Faced with a phalanx of old duffers who had already made up their minds, or who had had their minds made up for them by the chairman, I took my seat a few places away from Maurice. Both of us knew these men but somehow in this context they seemed strangers. Our chairman had chosen for his form of address a sort of lecture or harangue quoting salty expressions which were calculated to make the prudish Mrs Andrews blush to order and declaiming: 'Is this really the sort of language we want to hear on our stage!' He then went on to cite what he considered to be the subversive bits, quoting them out of context, editing them to suit his purpose, and claiming they could lead to civil unrest and even rioting. Finally he suggested that the scene with the mob leader should be removed altogether and the tragic ending deleted. I protested that he was exceeding his powers as chairman by interfering in artistic matters and that he was in no position to make alarmist claims about the script until he had seen the play performed on the stage. It was all to no avail; the board had been swayed.

My conviction was, and still is, that none of them had actually read the play. There simply would not have been time. The most likely scenario, though this is pure conjecture on my part, was that the chairman rang each board member in turn the previous evening and aired the same views he intended to elaborate upon at the meeting. The result, however, was a foregone conclusion. On a show of hands the motion that the production be cancelled without reservation was carried by six votes to two. Glancing to my right I saw that the other dissenting hand raised was that of Maurice O'Callaghan. We had not exchanged a single glance during the entire and painfully predictable proceedings but now we allowed ourselves a wry smile, happy in the knowledge that unlike the others we had not indulged in one word of collusion.

I have often thought over the years that Maurice, who came from a Catholic background and was to play the part of the threatened Catholic worker, and myself from a Protestant background, (who as well as directing the play was to take the part of the mob leader), virtually represented a metaphor for the play's non-sectarian stance; and here we were taking a mutual stand against a more insidious form of sectarianism, namely the withdrawal of the right to free speech. I do not believe that Maurice was given as much credit as he deserved at the time because too many people, including reporters speculated out of ignorance and he did not seem to them to be a major player. There were still a few matters to clear up and as I recall it I was invited to speak. I asked if they were aware of the company's liabilities in financial matters. Many of the people working on the production had been engaged on a freelance basis so this would not be covered by the company's regular wage bill. The author would expect six weeks royalties or more depending on the advance bookings (which were already looking healthy), and the designer had made models and drawings as well as starting work on the actual construction of the set. These and many other problems had to be addressed and as soon as possible. The chairman airily dismissed any claims by the freelance actors and indeed by the author on the grounds that a play that had not been performed could not be subject to royalties since it had produced no income; and the same principle applied to the freelance performers. What nonsense! As for the designer, he was sure that he and the company could reach some happy compromise. He was reckoning without Mr Henry Lynch Robinson, and I myself realised that I was dealing with an estate agent and not a theatre impressario. It was then I chose to announce that I would have to reconsider my position. Asked what I meant, I realised I had been playing for time and giving myself a chance to think. Pressed for an answer I came straight out with it: 'I'm offering my resignation as artistic director as from now,' I said. I could see straight away that this had the desired effect. Now the boot was on the other foot. The chairman's face was grim but regardless I pressed on: 'I am, however aware of the company's obligations to Bangor Borough Council's plans which I was instrumental in setting in motion.' These plans, now well advanced, were to run a summer season in their Little Theatre with an augmented Group Theatre Company. The Group Theatre's doors could be kept open during the lean months of June, July, August and a part of September, with the successes of a previous season I had run in Bangor with Betty Hogg and James Greene, while Bangor enjoyed the earlier offerings of the Belfast company which they almost certainly would not have seen. This plan I had put before the board some months earlier in my capacity as assistant artistic director and it had been welcomed enthusiastically and passed unanimously. Now was the time to turn this plan to my advantage. I did not think it fair or reasonable that Bangor should be involved in our differences, I said, and with the board's agreement I would remain to complete the theatre's dual programme until September. You could almost hear the communal sigh of relief as my offer was accepted. So unmindful were they of the theatre's overall programme and obligations that no-one had thought of putting it on the agenda, but at this point I reaffirmed that my resignation was immediate and unequivocal. The vice-chairman wondered if a form of words could be found that would be mutually agreed and might save face all round. This offer I declined but took the opportunity to suggest that Mr McMullan, as Head of Programmes at BBC Northern Ireland, had a conflict of interests in that his assessment of what was suitable for public broadcasting was at odds with his position as vice-chairman of the Group Theatre. He made some lame excuse about acting in the public interest. This was our final exchange and shortly afterwards I left the room with Maurice and went to meet the author and the cast.

As a footnote, I must emphasize that I was determined to honour my obligation to Bangor Borough Council. This factor, out of ignorance or a tendancy to generalise, theatre historians have tended to ignore. News is not news if it is not sensational.

II

The air in the crowded bar was expectant to put it mildly. The Elbow Room with its genial landlord, Charlie Lavery, its friendly head barman,

Gerry, and its comfortable snugs was virtually a home from home for the actors, and they were all waiting to hear the outcome of the meeting, not least Sam himself, who as the author of the play had most to lose. I came straight to the point. 'They've as good as banned your play Sam, by demanding changes that are clearly unacceptable. They want the mob scene cut, the ending changed – to what they didn't specify – and the language modified throughout the play to their requirements. Meanwhile the play is withdrawn indefinitely.'

'Not one word,' Sam thundered, 'I'll not change a word of it!'

'I thought you'd say that, Sam, that's why I've resigned.'

At the very mention of the word it seemed that everyone in the bar wanted to resign or hand in their notice. Obviously a few drinks had been consumed in our absence which no doubt accounted for the fervour of the protesting voices. That being said, it was not long before reports appeared that virtually the whole company had walked out; and that piece of 'mythology' persists to this very day. The truth is that neither I, nor the company, (on my advice) walked out *en masse*. Only the freelance performers which included John McBride, James Boyce and Charles Witherspoon, who in his wisdom the chairman thought were not necessary to pay, did I advise to ring Equity and take legal action (again on my advice and with the backing of J.G. Devlin), a move which along with Sam's threats to take a similar course, backed by well-articulated vocal protests, made serious headlines. I do not remember, perhaps because of its qualifications, that my own resignation caused much of a stir. Harold Goldblatt's resignation was, largely, I think because of a clash of personalities between himself and the chairman, Ritchie McKee.

My resignation was reported the following day stating the obvious reasons, together with the directors' defence of their position in a statement clearly worded by the chairman, giving the board's reasons for withdrawing the play in the public interest with hints of civil unrest, rioting and so on. It may be that he overplayed his hand a little for some commentators latched on to some of his more colourful claims with a degree of relish. For example, he described the play as 'full of grossly vicious phrases and situations which would undoubtedly offend and affront every section of the public,' adding, 'It is the policy of the Ulster Group Theatre to keep political and religious controversies off our stage.' 'The Troubles' were far in the future and Sam's plea for tolerance and brotherhood in the workplace was a prophetic warning of the dangers of sectarian bigotry; he was if anything a prophet of his times. *The Country Boy*, a fine first play, had opened on the 7th April so, if my memory serves me right, the story must have broke before the end of the month or the beginning of May and to be fair, the press gave more credence to our version of events. Jack Sayers, the editor, of the traditionally conservative *Belfast Telegraph*, virtually championed our cause, a stance he maintained for many months. This of course raised many dissident voices, in the correspondence columns and elsewhere, for censorship is a highly emotive issue. I myself remember my own cousin, later to become director of the Arts Council of Northern Ireland, writing a letter of protest, entirely unsolicited and with name and address supplied when Ritchie McKee's brother tried to add his weight to the fray. He wrote:

> "The Lord Mayor has said, 'There is no future for plays on a sectarian theme.' Further, 'Plays with a sectarian theme make it difficult for Lord Mayors and members of local authorities who are anxious to spend as much money as possible in promoting the arts.'
>
> "As a citizen of Belfast I must ask for the Lord Mayor's urgent assurance that these statements carry no implication of civic censorship or pressure; as they read, it is difficult to construe them otherwise."

Sam himself was not an individual to be easily silenced and he traded blow for blow with his detractors in the free-for-all that ensued.

48

Meanwhile back in The Elbow Room plans were being laid and plots hatched. We were all determined that Sam's play, unadulterated and unaltered should be staged in Belfast. But how? That was the question. It seemed that all doors would be closed against us. We had no company, no money and public funding was out of the question. I like to think that I kept a steady hand on the tiller at this time and I believe I did. Besides, I clearly had the loyalty of the company; but it was Henry Lynch Robinson who came up with the first really practical, positive suggestion. Naturally we were all ears and he had our undivided attention.

'It was really no problem forming a company,' he said, it was more a question of who wanted to be involved. Obviously Sam and myself were front-runners but neither of us had any money at the time. That didn't matter, Henry explained. Say the company was formed with a nominal capital of one thousand pounds, only a limited number of shares, say four hundred, need be taken up. Henry was willing to take up one hundred of these and he was sure Arthur Campbell of Campbell's Coffee Bar, another favourite rendezvous of the actors, would be willing to invest. That left Sam and myself. Sam suddenly remembered he had an insurance policy that he could cash in; and now it was down to me. I had recently moved into an expensive rented house in the fashionable Mount Charles and was finding it hard to make ends meet. I thought I might muster sixty pounds at the most. Charlie Lavery reached for his wallet and handed me a wad of notes. 'There's sixty to match your sixty,' he said. 'I don't want it back! Just put by four seats in the front row for me on the opening night. I wouldn't miss this for worlds!'

And so Ulster Bridge Productions was born, but where were we to find a theatre or even a venue that could be adapted to our requirements? Sam and myself crowded into public telephone kiosks to make what were to be abortive calls. Mr George Lodge of the Grand Opera House was 'unavailable' and his theatre was engaged for the

49

foreseeable future, which was not surprising since he was a close friend of Ritchie McKee and his brother, the Lord Mayor. All of them had been enraged by Tyrone Guthrie's production of Gerard McLarnon's *The Bonefire* staged there a year before its airing at the Edinburgh Festival. St Mary's Hall which had a not very workable platform rather than a stage was plainly apprehensive about the inflammatory content of the play as portrayed in the newspaper reports and gave us a cool reception. There seemed nowhere to turn; but some time later Jack Loudan, the former director of CEMA, turned up at The Elbow Room to inform us that he had withdrawn his play *Trouble in the Square* in protest at the banning of Sam's play and as an act of solidarity. *Trouble in the Square* was the third play announced in our press launch just a few weeks previously, so thanks to our board the entire programme had fallen apart, leaving me to pick up the pieces and form two companies to honour the Bangor and Group seasons.

Jack had some useful suggestions to make. Addressing me, he said, 'Why don't you ring Tony?' Jack Loudan was on first name terms with the world-famous theatre director, Tyrone Guthrie, and said he knew he was at home at his house Annaghmakerrig in County Monaghan. 'You won the Tyrone Guthrie scholarship and you were in Tony's production of *The Bonefire* last year. I'm sure he can give you the right advice. His number, easy to remember, is Newbliss 3, and you can say I gave it to you. Ring when you're ready.' I have not forgotten that number to this day.

I do not recall whether it was on this occasion or at a later meeting that Jack also suggested I should call on Frank Reynolds, the genial manager of the Empire Theatre which stood in Victoria Square until the early 1960s.

I knew little of Frank Reynolds at this time other than Jack Loudan's encouraging report that he was friendly and approachable, so, although not daring to hope for too much, I approached the interview with little trepidation. I cannot over emphasise that neither at this stage, nor at any other, did Sam or Henry Lynch Robinson take part in any negotiations, despite persistent reports to the contrary.

The old Empire Theatre of Varieties, formerly a Music Hall, had celebrated its diamond jubilee in 1955 but was now in a parlous state. The brown paintwork was peeling and the previously plush seating was now worn and faded. Nevertheless, as I crept into the auditorium I experienced a sense of former grandeur, as well I might, for many famous names had appeared here, including Marie Lloyd, Harry Lauder, Jimmy O'Dea and Charlie Chaplin. I could envisage Sam's play on that stage with a house full of shipyard workers happy in their surroundings. I went to the box office and asked if Mr Reynolds was in the building. 'He's in his office,' was the reply, 'Can I say who's calling?' 'The name's Ellis, Jimmy Ellis,' I replied, and in a couple of minutes I was sitting face to face with Frank. 'I think I know why you've come', he said, and we got straight down to business. 'Jack Loudan tells me you've formed a company.' 'Yes, with Sam Thompson, Henry Lynch Robinson and Arthur Campbell of Campbell's coffee bar.' 'Well that's a good start,' said Frank.

'Our directors are waiting to hear from you. Our chairman, Mr Dermot Findlater, has been made aware of the controversy and has asked to see a copy of the play.' I could not believe my ears! After so many apparently closed doors here was one that seemed to be wide open. I still feel slightly ashamed that I had overlooked this rather shabby old theatre with its repertoire of fourth-rate variety and murky touring shows such as *Soldiers in Skirts*. Suddenly it became a place of glamour and excitement. A theatre is a theatre and a stage is a stage; and this was a proper theatre! I could not wait for Frank to show me round; but first there was a telephone call to make. Frank got through to his chairman and was soon engaged in animated conversation. 'I've got Jimmy Ellis in the office,' I heard him say, 'and although we haven't got around to discussing it yet, I think he might be interested in staging Sam Thompson's play in our theatre.' Naturally I nodded in agreement, then turning to me, Frank said, 'The chairman of the company that owns the theatre wants to meet you in Dublin with the script; you can come with me on my next visit; all our expenses will be taken care of.' I cannot describe my elation at this point but I knew we were on the first rung of the ladder.

Now Frank took me on a conducted tour of the entire theatre; stalls, circle, gallery, boxes, backstage, wings, flies, dressing rooms, cyclorama, dressing rooms and artiste's bar. I compared it with the poor facilities of our little Group Theatre and realised there was no comparison; I knew then and there that Sam's play would be far better off being staged here where we were standing and was already envisaging a production on a much larger scale. When we reached centre stage, Frank recalled Charlie Chaplin's telegram sent from Switzerland for the night of the Diamond Jubilee and read out on the occasion presumably by Mr Dermot Findlater. As far as I am aware Frank remembered it virtually verbatim:

"My best wishes to the Friends of the Belfast Empire Theatre of Varieties on its Diamond Jubilee. May you enjoy long years of peace, prosperity and happiness."

It seemed like a good omen, not only for Sam's play, but for the future of the theatre itself. 'By the way,' Frank said as we took leave of each other, 'perhaps you could let me have two or three scripts of the play in the meantime. It might speed things up.' I was only too happy to oblige.

I reported the good news back to my co-directors, Sam and Henry but advised caution until the Dublin directors had the chance to read the play; they did not have to wait long. Within a week Frank Reynolds let it be known that he was ready to see me and I responded straight away. When he opened his office door, the broad smile said it all. 'I've read the play and so have the directors in Dublin including Mr Findlater and his managing director John McGrail and we are all agreed that the

52

play should be staged in our theatre. There will of course be a few formalities which should be ironed out at the next board meeting which takes place in a week's time and which we are requested to attend. This was what I meant by speeding things up,' he added with a benign smile. From then on Frank and myself were to form a bond which would last for some time. We raised a glass to the play's success in the old Kitchen Bar opposite the Empire's stage door and then I went off in search of Sam who was waiting anxiously for news. 'They've accepted your play' I said, 'subject to formalities,' but Sam was on cloud nine and didn't even question the proviso. I think by this time we trusted each other completely and this trust I believe lasted until events overtook us both. I don't think the news broke at this time because we met in the Crown Bar with its quiet snugs and by now had learned to be discreet.

Discretion was important to avoid the next twist in the story and jump the next hurdle. Harry McMullan sent a message that he would like to see me in the BBC boardroom and I duly went. After pouring me a drink he hinted darkly that I should consider my own future. I was a family man with a promising career ahead of me and both he and the chairman thought highly of my prospects. Was it worth throwing it all away for a play whose author refused to listen to reason? However, in spite of everything, the chairman was willing to hold another meeting to see if we could patch up our differences and reach a compromise. Sam would of course be invited and the meeting would take place at the chairman's rather grand house on the fashionable Malone Road. Knowing the strength of our position I advised Sam to accompany me to this meeting, anxious to learn how much ground they were prepared to give, and he agreed. It was a beautiful evening in late May and on arrival we were conducted to a sunny verandah and offered gins and tonic. It wasn't exactly our tipple but I guess we were too overawed to refuse, which no doubt was the intention. 'Now gentlemen,' Ritchie began, (a form of address which I believe was calculated to embarrass us further), 'I'm sure we can find a solution to our difficulties.' Sam and I exchanged looks wondering what to expect next. 'Would you, Sam,' he continued, 'be prepared to sit down with Mr McMullan, Jimmy, and myself and go through your script line by line deleting really offensive expressions and modifying rather than cutting the entire mob scene?' It was a clear case of dividing to conquer and I could see Sam's expression hardening to a mask. 'I trust Jimmy as the director to take care of these things and he always consults me, but the mob scene and tragic ending are essential to the plot; and alterations were made before we went into rehearsal.' 'I question your right or your qualifications to interfere in these matters,' I added, knowing we were in a strong position, but the debate continued, going round in circles and getting nowhere as Mr McKee plied us with more gin and hoped we would 'see reason'. The whole discussion ground to a halt as Ritchie and his vice-chairman sought to reach a compromise and save face. Eventually everyone ran out of steam and we took our leave with Sam not quite sure what our position was.

As we walked down the rather imposing drive in the dark Sam asked me if anything had changed. 'No Sam,' I replied, guessing he was a little fuddled, 'nothing has changed.' 'In that case I'm going to water his rhododendrons.' 'I'll join you,' I said.

III

As we passed through the gates Sam said, 'Let's go and have a proper drink,' and we crossed the road and set off for the nearby Botanic Inn to review the situation. We discussed Harold Goldblatt's resignation earlier in the month, (May 12th); he was the founder of the Group Theatre and my former boss. He had called the withdrawal of the play 'a major blunder'. McKee's riposte included the absurd suggestion that he would like to see the play printed in its present form so that the public might judge for themselves, thereby showing his complete ignorance of the theatre's modus operandi and how unfit he was for the powerful positions he held in that field.

An example of wholly misinformed speculation appeared at the same time from an unnamed *Belfast Telegraph* reporter who was either looking for a story or trying to be helpful. He wrote:

> "Stanley Ilsley and Leo McCabe, the owners of the Olympia Theatre Dublin, are understood to be interested in presenting *Over The Bridge* in Belfast and Dublin with an Ulster cast. They have presented a number of plays in Belfast and would probably stage *Over The Bridge* at the Grand Opera House where they have formerly appeared."

The article ended with the statement: 'Mr Thompson has been in Dublin for the past few days.'

The entire suggestion was ridiculous though in the end it proved to be ironic. Here were Sam and I sitting in the Botanic Inn and I was the one who was Dublin bound in less than a week. The mention of the Opera House was downright laughable, for if there was anyone in the city who wouldn't touch Sam's play with a barge pole it was Mr George Lodge, the proprietor or lessee of the said Grand Opera House.

It was getting late, or more likely they had called 'Time' and we decided to call it a day. As we walked down the Malone Road I reassured Sam, not for the first time, that everything was going to plan. By this time next week everything should be in order and we would know exactly where we stood, if everything turned out as I anticipated. There was one thing more I wished to confide in Sam and that was Jack Loudan's suggestion that we should consult Tyrone Guthrie. It was my intention, I said, to offer him the job of directing the play whilst I would remain as producer. Sam was appalled but I said we could talk about it all when I came back from Dublin. We had reached Botanic Gardens and Elmwood Avenue and I suspected Sam might be going to the Arts Club. Not for the first time, I advised caution and discretion in what he might let slip; for the whole town, and especially the arts community were agog with curiosity and I warned Sam to stay tight-lipped about any developments, especially our meeting with Ritchie and Harry and my impending trip to Dublin. I felt strongly that keeping our cards close to our chest was vital every step of the way. On that note we parted. With regard to tactics, I had personally rejected the idea of any kind of forum or public debate on the whole issue of censorship, choosing to have the play, when eventually staged, speak for itself.

Perhaps it was because of this reticence on our part, that the arts magazine *Threshold*, edited by Mary O'Malley, opted to hold a forum of its own, with contributions from John Lewis-Crosby, the then director of CEMA, Janet McNeil, writer and dramatist, the poet Roy McFadden and Mary O'Malley herself, who was at that time noteworthy for running a theatre in her own front room and presenting the verse plays of W.B. Yeats. Lewis-Crosby's article was headed 'CEMA and the Professional Theatre.' And it contained some well-chosen, 'off the cuff' words which I shall quote verbatim:

"What of the future? Here I must speak my own views, which are not necessarily those of CEMA. In Ulster we have two companies from which we could expect great things if the opportunities are offered to them. In fact there is no reason why Belfast should not be recognised in time as the centre for drama in Ireland. If we can convince the Government and local authorities that theatre is the right of every citizen as are public libraries, museums, parks, etc., then the rest will follow."

None of these contributors had consulted either Sam Thompson or myself, nor I presume each other before penning their articles though John Lewis-Crosby had attended (as an 'assessor' without a vote) the board meeting which had overseen the banning of the play and somewhat reluctantly I believe had been obliged to accept my resignation as artistic director. My lasting impression of that fateful board meeting was that Lewis-Crosby was very uncomfortable and distinctly embarrassed by the entire proceedings and in fact he was to tell me some years later that he felt his hands were tied and that he, personally, did not agree with the board's ruling. By this time he was no longer director of CEMA and in the interim I had heard of growing tensions between Lewis-Crosby and his chairman, Ritchie McKee, amounting to a distinct cooling off in their day to day relationship. I do believe, though I have no evidence to substantiate this notion, that John Lewis-Crosby was instrumental in securing my appointment as assistant director of productions at the Group Theatre in the early summer of the year 1957. Prior to that date, in 1955 I think, he had, on behalf of CEMA, offered financial aid, along with a provincial tour, to the New Theatre Bangor which was run under the joint directorship of myself, James Greene and Betty Hogg. This company was at the time a serious threat to the established Belfast theatres and notably introduced to the professional ranks a number of young actors, among them Julian Glover and Colin Blakely, who was to become a protégé of Laurence Olivier.

I will briefly summarise the comments of other contributors to that forum in *Threshold* magazine: Janet McNeill made two comments which seem strangely incongruous, especially as they follow each other in the same paragraph. They are: 'A community in whom the love of the drama is so deep-seated will not require state aid for its theatre,' followed by, 'No theatre should be the vehicle either for State propaganda or for the propaganda of its opposition.' It is worth pointing out, I think, that she had not yet seen the play, nor it is to be presumed, read the script.

The poet, Roy McFadden was more perceptive, I think, and certainly more witty:

"Censors never see themselves as enemies of freedom. They appear to themselves as wise fathers removing dangerous toys from the inexperienced hands of eager children … The other day I discussed the banning of *Over The Bridge* with a man who is intelligent, sincere and tolerant in most things. He cracked under the pressure of argument and asserted that the playwright (known to him only as the author of a suppressed play) was in all probability a communist. In other words an enemy … as a citizen, with my taxes paid, rates paid, vote ready for a worthy candidate, I suggest to the Group Theatre chairman and his friends that they risk becoming figures of fun to future generations."

Mary O'Malley summed up the debate in an otherwise uninformed contribution: 'The present management is, no doubt, well meaning, but it will inevitably learn that a living theatre is not purchasable merchandise.'

But to return to our top-secret plans, I vividly remember the excitement of that first Dublin trip; it was to be the first of many. Frank Reynolds and myself (Sam was not involved at this stage, nor would he meet the Dublin directors until the opening night), travelled by train, the famous *Enterprise*, whose main feature apart from its speed was the stop at Goraghwood. Here Customs officials came on board to regulate the sale of drinks and tobacco. From now on these were virtually half price as we were now in the Free State rather than Northern Ireland and the temptation to go to the crowded bar was all but irresistible, though Frank advised caution, as the Findlater hospitality was legendary. This I would discover long before the day was ended. However, Frank, a convivial man by nature, led the way along the corridor and bought the first drink while I topped up my supply of Gallagher's cigarettes. In what seemed like no time at all we arrived at Amiens Street station and had boarded a taxi bound for 'Findlater's Corner' as it was called. At the far end of O'Connell Street where it joins Upper O'Connell Street, it was then one of Dublin's most famous landmarks and the taxi stopped without hesitation. 'This is all on the firm,' said Frank, as he paid the fare and asked for a receipt.

I think I was impressed rather than overawed as I entered the building. After a brief look around I was taken up to the first floor and introduced to the chairman, Mr Dermot Findlater, and his managing director, Mr John McGrail. We shook hands warmly and my welcome was unequivocal. 'Come into the office, Jimmy,' said Dermot, ushering me through a solid oak door. 'We're expecting a few others but not many. Mary, she's the company secretary, will be along shortly and then we'll attend to the formalities. They should be pretty straightforward since we're all 'reading from the same script,' he added with a knowing wink and we got down to business straight away.

To be honest, I don't recall many details about what happened in that office except for some astonishing developments that were to be of some consequence for Ulster Bridge Productions. The commercial dealings of Findlater & Company were dealt with first and fairly swiftly, then attention was focused on the play and its immediate future. To my astonishment it was proposed that I should be given three hundred ordinary shares which was the minimum requirement apparently for me to become a director of the firm. This, it was felt, would forge a link between the two companies and facilitate communication when it came to drawing up a contract. Of course my first loyalty would be as artistic director of Ulster Bridge Productions, but they felt sure there should be no conflict of interest when I heard what was on offer.

Firstly, the play was accepted as written and without reservations. No cuts or alterations would be suggested either in Belfast or in Dublin where it was hoped I might find a management company to stage it on the strength of its expected success at the Empire. Secondly, Findlaters would cover pre-production costs and guarantee us against loss from advance bookings. Thereafter Findlaters would take 40 per cent of the box office receipts. I cannot vouch for the accuracy of these figures after a half century but they were generous terms which I knew myself and my co-directors would not and could not refuse. It was understood that I would report back to them and then contracts would be signed. We were, in effect, from that moment committed and there would be no turning back.

A celebration lunch followed to cement our new partnership, though I was to learn that such lunches were a regular feature of the Findlater routine, used to tasting newly imported wines and occasionally other Findlater products such as charcuterie and cheese. The main courses however, were prepared by an excellent German cook, a charming lady who made her appearance at the end of the meal to enquire if everything was to Mr Findlater's satisfaction, which needless to say it was. It was on this occasion that I met Alex Findlater, a pleasant young man and the son and heir who was being brought up in the family business and was really proud of its history and traditions. He was to write a book many years later, *Findlaters: The Story of a Dublin Merchant Family*, (2001), in which he traces the entire history of the Empire Theatre of Varieties and, most interestingly, highlighting the climax and outcome of the *Over The Bridge* controversy with more accuracy than most commentators.

After a fine vintage port we all shook hands warmly and I left the building with Frank, walking on air. 'Well that went well,' he said, beaming broadly. 'I think we can call it Mission Accomplished,' I replied, as we walked down O'Connell Street to clear our heads; and I remember thinking to myself how easy and cushy it was to be a theatre producer and entrepreneur. Little did I realise that I still had a lot to learn.

Back in Belfast, Sam was elated at the news. I had called round to his house at 55 Craigmore Street to deliver the good tidings immediately on arrival; now it was only a matter of approving and signing contracts and the terms were very much in our favour. I suggested we should call on Henry Lynch Robinson at his office in May Street and this we did. Right away we showed him the draft terms and he was very impressed. 'You've done extremely well, James' he said, beaming broadly. 'Now I can get ahead with my designs and new ground plan without further delay. I've already taken the liberty of asking Frank Reynolds if I could measure up on the strength of what you told me before your Dublin trip and I've already done that, but I imagine secrecy is still essential until we're ready to launch our press release.' Then he added wickedly, 'The Bourgeois Gentilhomme will go through the roof of course when he hears the news; he was absolutely determined the play would not have an airing in Belfast and here it is, being staged in a proper theatre without public funding and without his blessing!' Henry had no time for middle class morality or the pretentious snobbery which accompanied it; nor indeed for the misuse of power. To him, Ritchie McKee epitomised all these failings.

Henry Lynch Robinson was a remarkable man. A self-confessed homosexual in the days when it was illegal and the word 'gay' had not been coined, he had said so at the very outset of our enterprise. Guessing that I probably knew, he had addressed himself mainly to Sam, probably not knowing what the reaction of this patently heterosexual ex-shipyard worker would be. As we joined forces in the Elbow Room he had made his position quite clear when he said, 'Just so as you know, I am a homosexual; but it will never interfere, either directly or indirectly, in our working relationship.' 'That's okay by me Henry', said Sam shaking hands warmly, and the subject was never mentioned again.

Meanwhile a little celebration was in order and we retired to a bar known as the Garrick which, Henry thought, might be even older than the Empire. Here we raised our glasses to each other, to the play and even to our arch enemy Ritchie, who, we thought, might prove to be more responsible for the success of the play than he could ever have foreseen. The Belfast public did not like to be told what it should see or should not see and curiosity is a great crowd puller. Besides, the publicity seemed to be going all our way with cartoonists, including my dear friend, the late Rowel Friers, having a field day. At some point Sam mentioned that I was thinking of offering the direction of the play to Tyrone Guthrie but Henry, like Sam, thought this would be a mistake. This was a David and Goliath scenario, he said, and it was essential I took the role of David. Nevertheless as Guthrie was a sort of mentor at the time I felt I should consult him and so I rang Newbliss 3.

Around this time and occasionally since, I have been asked a number of questions about the great man. What was the importance of Guthrie? What was he like as a director? For a start, I tremble to think what sort of career I would have had if I had not won the Tyrone Guthrie Scholarship, the only one of its kind awarded at this time, or indeed at any other, as a result of which I was the first student from Northern Ireland to attend a drama school for many years after. Kenneth Branagh springs to mind, but he was largely brought up in England and attended RADA, I believe on a scholarship. My one experience of Guthrie as a director was in a play called *The Bonefire* by Gerard McLarnon where I played the part of Davy Marr, a sidekick and general dogsbody to J.G. Devlin as the militant Orangeman, Davy Mitchell. *The Bonefire* was to represent Belfast at the 1958 Edinburgh Festival after its premiere at the Grand Opera House Belfast attended by many prominent citizens including Ritchie McKee and his brother the mayor, Alderman Cecil McKee. His photograph, in full regalia, appeared prominently with other European mayors on the fully illustrated programme of events at Edinburgh and McLarnon's play apparently caused much offence. Ritchie McKee, was obviously so overawed by the man he addressed as 'Dr. Guthrie' that he asked Harold Goldblatt, then still the Artistic Director, to make certain changes. Harry, in turn was apprehensive of approaching the great man, but according to J.G. Devlin, he muttered something about the chairman trying to interfere. 'That's entirely a matter for you', Guthrie replied, 'but if changes are made you can take my name off the programme'. That was the end of the matter.

I remember the rehearsals for *The Bonefire* vividly in which the modus operandi differed widely from the approach of Hugh Hunt where I made my English debut with the young Prunella Scales. Firstly, Guthrie insisted that everyone was 'off the book' and word perfect by the first day. There was no preamble of any kind except the briefest of verbal sketches of the position of the bonefire, a background of streets, entrances and exits running off to right and left.

'Now,' he said, clapping his hands together – a gesture which I was to get used to – 'who begins the piece?' 'That's us,' said Jimmy Devlin, rising to his feet and taking up a position roughly right of centre as I joined him. I whispered nervously to J.G. 'Where do we stand?' 'Stand wherever the hell you like,' he replied. 'I'm standin' here!' Well, not knowing where to go, I stood beside him when again I heard the handclap and a voice said, 'Begin.' It was Jimmy who had the opening lines which were as I remember a string of orders followed by the words, 'Do you understand?' which were followed by a nod of the head. My answer was, 'Yes, Davy.' which I too delivered with a nod of the head. Jimmy, feeling the need to move, went over to examine the bonefire in detail and I, full of questions, followed him wherever he went, stopping to face him at regular intervals and bobbing and weaving in imitation of my role model. It seemed to go on forever and I was sure I was for the sack. The scene reached a point where the character of Davy Mitchell runs out of patience and demands, 'Have I not already told you what I want you to do first?' This, he emphasised with a nod and I, nodding back replied, 'Yes, Mr Mitchell.' 'Then go and do it, d'ye understand?' (Another nod). Having finally got the message, I answered with a nod, 'Yes, Mr Mitchell.'

At this point there was the now familiar handclap and the tall figure of Tyrone Guthrie was placing his hands on our shoulders. 'Now then,' he said, 'you remind me of two budgerigars, the old budgie and the young budgie. I think we can build on that,' and this he proceeded to do, improvising variations on our creativity. All in all, I learned a great deal from being so closely involved in this production, though I was not ready to risk his uncanny powers of improvisation. My part was more than just a cameo and I was involved in most of the action. I noted with relief that he was very kind to young actors, among whom were myself and Colin Blakely, and this father figure continued to exert his benign influence when we moved to Edinburgh. Our venue was the Lyceum Theatre where we were preceded by T.S. Eliot's *The Elder Statesman* starring Paul Rogers. At an onstage rehearsal where he was adding some finishing touches to his production, Guthrie asked me if I could run a four minute mile. Realising that he was joking I replied that I didn't think so but said I was pretty nippy over four hundred yards. 'That's good enough for me,' he replied with a smile. 'Well,' he continued, 'when J.G. sends you on one of these endless errands, I want you to exit downstage right, go through the pass door, find your way to the second tier box, run past and all the way round the back of the upper circle; again find the pass door and reappear on cue at downstage left, out of breath and with your mission accomplished.' 'Yes, I can do that,' I replied confidently. 'Try it now,' he said with a smile, and I'll time you.' I set off at a gallop and reappeared as instructed. 'Nearly perfect,' he said. 'If anything you were a little early; but that's no bad thing. You can always pant quietly until you hear your cue and if you're late because of some unforeseen circumstance, I'm sure Jimmy will welcome the opportunity to improvise.' He always, I remember, endeavoured to make rehearsals fun.

That's just a couple of examples of Guthrie's creativity. Another was when the actor John McBride, balancing a lambeg drum on his stomach, presumed to ask him where he should stand during a crowd scene, the great man replied, 'Oh just hang around where you are. If I've done my job properly, nobody will be looking at you; all eyes will be on the lady with the pram, pushing her way through the throng.'

Now for a further insight into his role as an early mentor. One afternoon, when there was a matinee of *The Elder Statesman* at the Lyceum, we had a half day off. Hanging about at that end of Prince's Street, I spotted Guthrie and his wife at a hot dog stall. As usual he was wearing a suit with tennis shoes which may have been incongruous but were comfortable. He called me over and asked me if I would like a hot dog, adding that he and Judith had a box at the Lyceum to see the Eliot play and would I care to join them. Of course I jumped at the chance and we strolled up Lothian Street past the Usher Hall and took our seats in plenty of time. As always, Tyrone Guthrie was punctual. At the end of the performance he turned to me and asked what I thought of the play and when I hesitated he said with a smile, 'come on, you're the Eliot expert.' My mind was racing. 'What could he possibly mean?' Then the penny dropped. He must have kept tabs on my progress at Bristol and somehow heard of my production of *The Cocktail Party* at the university. I floundered somewhat but managed to blurt out that I thought it was inferior to *The Confidential Clerk*, *The Family Reunion*, the early *Murder in the Cathedral* and *The Cocktail Party*. 'Ah', he said with another benign smile, 'I was waiting for that ...' then, 'come on, let's go round and sympathise with Paul.' Paul Rogers had paid several visits to Belfast with what must have been The Royal Shakespeare Company and one role I remember clearly was Macbeth in which he gave a superb performance. On each occasion he sought me out at the Arts Club and I can only put down our friendship at this time to Guthrie's introduction.

It cannot be stressed enough that Tyrone Guthrie was both a maverick and probably the most world famous director of his time. Taking into account that he was a compulsive globe trotter, the phrase 'most world famous' is not an overstatement, or as James Forsyth in the prologue to his biography puts it: "Anti-Broadway, anti-West End, anti-everything implied in the term 'Legitimate Theatre', he ended up with a legitimate claim to the title of most important British born theatre director of his time…" His range was enormous: from the Old Vic in London, where, under his formidable producer Lilian Baylis, he engaged Laurence Olivier, John Gielguid and Charles Laughton, among others to Elsinore, Denmark, where Olivier played Hamlet and Vivien Leigh played Ophelia, then, on to the opera *Carmen* at Sadler's Wells and the Metropolitan, New York, his hunger was insatiable. He directed the celebrated Habima Company – the National Theatre of Israel - persuaded Alec Guinness and Irene Worth to star in the inaugural production of 'Richard III' at Stratford, Ontario and ten years later he founded the Guthrie Theatre Minneapolis. In spite of this he never forgot his roots and his Annaghmakkerig house near Newbliss, County Monaghan, was a treasured retreat. His professional career had virtually begun at the Northern Ireland BBC after a spell at the newly formed Oxford Playhouse. He had a love affair, however, with the Group Theatre Company who in my time were all mature performers. He formed a company to perform at the Festival of Britain which consisted entirely of Group Theatre players and a chosen work was *The Passing Day* by George Sheils, a proven success in the Group's repertoire. It starred Joseph Tomelty, who was spotted by one of the most powerful agents in London and launched on a highly successful film career.

When Guthrie answered my phone call, he was most cordial and anxious to catch up with all the news, especially after his confrontation the previous year over *The Bonefire*, another play that had stirred up controversy when it was presented, under his direction, at the Grand Opera House. 'Bring the script and the author with you,' he said. I pointed out that I didn't have a driving licence so my cousin Kenneth would have to drive us. He was certainly in an expansive mood and my wife Betty was also invited. 'Make a day of it and all stay for lunch,' he said. 'We don't get many visitors here.'

When we reached the centre of Monaghan town we saw a group of youths sitting on the steps of a fountain and my wife in her posh RADA accent, asked for directions from one of them. 'Can you point us in the direction of Newbliss,' she enquired, adding foolishly, 'my man.' 'Certainly missus,' was the reply as he sent us in exactly the opposite direction. My cousin, having driven round the town and found the relevant signpost, leaned over as he passed them again and said good-naturedly, 'Thanks boys.'

Presently we arrived at Newbliss and the imposing fading mansion of Annaghmakerrig where the Guthries were waiting to greet us. Sam was introduced as were Betty and Kenneth and then Tony suggested, since it was a fine day, that he and I should take a stroll round the lake while his wife Judith looked after the others. Sam was not invited to accompany us.

Guthrie asked me to take him through the entire story step by step, starting with the withdrawal of the play from rehearsal and my subsequent resignation, which of course was my reason for ringing him. I began by describing the furore that followed and the controversy in the newspapers, indicating that the reporting, though sometimes inaccurate, was by and large fair, and generally on our side. I also told him that Sam, myself and our designer had formed a company and through Jack Loudan I had discovered that the proprietors of the Belfast Empire were a Dublin company with which we had reached a happy agreement to stage the play in their theatre, though this could not happen for some time due to my obligations to the Bangor season, which I had been instrumental in setting up. Finally I asked him if, having read the script of course, he would consider directing the play, though the Opera House was now out of the question. 'Well that's probably my fault,' he said with a grin, going on to comment that as I had resigned on a matter of principle, the positive riposte would be better coming from me. Naturally I took it that he would not make a final decision until he had read the play. The lunch was not a memorable one in the culinary sense. The Guthrie household did not employ a cordon bleu cook and the main course consisted of boiled meat, with watery cabbage, over-cooked carrots and mashed potatoes, all no doubt from the vegetable garden. This was followed by a crumble of some sort with custard topped by a blob of the Guthrie home-produced jam; the Guthries had a small jam factory of which they were extremely proud. Lunch over, Tony suggested that I might care to dry the dishes as he washed up and so the table was cleared as he and I retired to the kitchen. This, I soon realised, was so that we could pick up the conversation by the lake where we had left off, and still out of earshot of the others. I remember thinking to myself that Tyrone Guthrie was a born conspirator; but to be honest I remember little, of that conversation. What I do recall is that he seemed quite fired up by my enthusiasm for the play and was very taken by the direct and open personality of its author, the gist of what the maestro had to say to his protégé was, 'Stand up for what you believe in.' 'Identify and confront the problems.' 'Recognise flaws and anticipate counter moves.' 'Resolutely oppose interference but have your own defences in good battle order.' He said he would clarify all this he said in a letter. On second thoughts, that lunch with the Guthries was probably the most, if not the most memorable one of my entire life, and to be truthful Sam and myself were not exactly used to 'haute cuisine'.

We re-joined the others just as it was time to go. We were escorted outside to where Ken had parked his car but before we said our thank-yous and goodbyes, Judith Guthrie had gathered together some parting gifts. These consisted of flowers, fresh eggs and pots of the Guthrie home-made jam. And so we took our leave and set off through Monaghan town on our way back to Belfast, taking care however, to stop for a favourably priced tipple on the Free State side of the border.

IV

Guthrie's long letter arrived within a day or two and though I was half expecting it, to my disappointment, he declined my hopeful suggestion that he might direct the play. His letter, reading between the lines, gave the impression that he did not think *Over The Bridge* was as good an effort as McLarnon's *The Bonefire*, but for all its faults, I did not share this view and privately doubted the great man's judgement. However, he did have some positive, constructive criticisms to make. Cuts and alterations were vital, he said, together with the removal of red herrings and references to characters not actually appearing in the action; above all, his considered opinion was to get rid of the women. As he put it forcefully: 'This is a man's play. Get the women's auxiliary to hell out of it!' I did not agree with him about the cutting of the women's roles though of course it was basically a problem or conflict of men in the workplace. The fact remained however, that the women at home were the ultimate victims, as the final scene of Sam's play so vividly and movingly illustrated.

However, before graciously and tactfully turning down our 'kind offer,' he remarked on the immediacy of the intuitive stand I had taken and shrewdly pointed out that as I had shown my belief in the play from the outset and in the integrity and honesty of its author, I must not only produce, but also direct the play. He went on to say that if we did not hasten to bring forward the production date, postponement could lead to loss of momentum. Nine months was a long delay and the press could be fickle. To put it bluntly, we were likely to go off like a damp squib and McKee and company would have the last laugh. On a cautionary note, he warned, 'Do not make the play your flag and cause,' (this last sentence betraying his doubts). Then he wrote in bold capital letters:

"YOU ARE RESIGNING BECAUSE OF CENSORSHIP." (underlined), "UNOFFICIAL." (underlined twice), "BY THE

ESTABLISHMENT." (underlined three times).

There was a final sentence, almost by way of a postscript:
"You may read my letter to Sam, or not, as you see fit, but read all of my letter or none of it. DO NOT EDIT ME!"

In a review of the Tyrone Guthrie Lecture which I had been invited to deliver in November, 1992, the *Belfast Newsletter's* reporter began with an amusing suggestion. He wrote, 'If and when Jimmy Ellis's autobiography appears, I have a title: *Washing the Dishes with Tony*.' Later in the article he went on in a more serious vein: 'That appalling interference with artistic freedom by CEMA, forerunner of the Arts Council, and others who had arrogated to themselves the right to be the arbiters of what should and should not be staged in Ulster ...' 'For the first time, Jimmy, at the core of that ghastly affair, (the *Over The Bridge* controversy) has spoken publicly about actions he despised and in opposition to which he put his own neck on the block.'

What a difference three decades had made! 'The Troubles' were still with us but had no direct link with Sam Thompson's play apart from the predictable undercurrent of sectarian bigotry which Sam had foreseen; and at least, freedom of expression for the playwright was now taken for granted.

Back to June, 1959 and I'm afraid to say I did edit Tony Guthrie's letter for the benefit of Sam and Henry though I passed on the more constructive criticisms, leaving no doubt in Sam's mind that the play needed a lot of 'cuts, alterations and re-structuring, together with the removal of red herrings and references to characters not actually appearing in the action.'

I told Sam that I agreed with these suggestions, but not the one which recommended the removal of the women's parts. I read the relevant passages of Guthrie's letter aloud, which said firstly, 'This is a man's play ...' which pleased Sam, and secondly, 'get the women's auxiliary to hell out of it ...' which made both Sam and Henry laugh. I think I chose this moment to tell them that Tyrone Guthrie had declined to direct the play and gave his reasons, but they showed no desire to have the letter read out in full, so the question never arose. However, both men seemed relieved that the matter had been settled once and for all, though it had not of course occurred to me at the time that had Guthrie accepted the offer, he would most likely have brought in his own preferred designer, Tanya Moiseiwitsch, all Henry's preparatory sketches would have been scrapped. As for Sam, the idea of cutting the women's parts would have appalled him. Anyway, now we all knew where we stood.

From then on I had to concentrate on my obligations to the Group Theatre's Belfast and Bangor seasons and I remember that I engaged further 'regulars' – mainly members of the previous company I had run in Bangor – with the addition of that fine actor, Colin Blakely, who I had persuaded to turn professional and who gave a wonderful performance in William Inge's play, *Picnic*. I do not now recall many details of that dual commitment and I have little by way of memorabilia to jog my memory beyond a few cuttings and the odd programme, price sixpence, for to be honest every spare moment was spent with Sam, lying on the floor of his front room surrounded by pages of his script and working on an entire re-draft of his play to suit the larger theatre. I hasten to add that none of these changes would have appeased Messrs McKee and McMullan, but Henry was consulted at regular intervals to keep abreast of possible new acting areas.

It was around this time that Sam must have taken a step that I was then unaware of, and the consequences of which must have disappointed him. For whatever reason, and he probably did not want to weaken my resolve or dampen my enthusiasm, but, without telling me, he sent a copy of *Over The Bridge* to the editor of the *Belfast Telegraph*, John E. 'Jack' Sayers. A copy of Sayers's reply exists in the newspaper's archives and was dug out by Maura Megaghy when she was researching material for a doctorate on Sam Thompson's life and work; she has subsequently written a book. I have recently come across Jack Sayers's letter to Sam, which Maura must have sent me, but I have no recollection of reading it then or since. Its content I think throws some light on the guarded attitude of a newspaper editor and is worth quoting at length:

"From John E. Sayers, *Belfast Telegraph*. 30 June 1959.

Dear Sam,

I want to thank you for allowing me to read the script, in which I recognise not only the authentic speech of the yards, but your ambition to show what manner of people we have here in Belfast and the stresses that beset them.

However, I must be frank and say that the play strikes me as being too extreme for presentation by the Group. As you know, I hold no special brief for the board, but I have to acknowledge that its position calls for greater selectivity than say, the Arts (Theatre). The mistake, I believe, was made by Ellis in committing the theatre without consulting his principals on what was obviously a matter for them.

But please do not think I am advocating the suppression of your work. I think the play is one that should be produced by an experimental theatre, if such there is in Belfast. Certainly, I hope you will still be able to find someone to stage it, so that the public can judge for themselves.

I respect your opinion so much that I am disturbed by the possibilities the play suggests. I had hoped that with the passage of time such antagonisms were abating, and that more and more ordinary Belfast people can be relied upon to keep their heads. I know that anything can happen with mob psychology, but we have been fortunate in escaping trouble for such a long time …"

In this letter Jack Sayers shows himself to be a reasonable man and, in a sense, something of a prophet in foreseeing troubles ahead, though there has been no evidence that they were in any way brought about by Sam's play; all that was still far in the future and in fact churches, both Protestant and Catholic, were to hail *Over The Bridge* as a plea for tolerance.

Reading between the lines, however, the letter betrays the mind of the natural equivocator. On the one hand it says, 'As you know, I hold no brief for the board,' and on the other, 'The mistake, I believe, was made by Ellis in committing the theatre without consulting his principals on what was obviously a matter for them.'

How are we to reconcile those two statements? In resigning I had shown my own lack of confidence in the board and had never regarded them as 'my principals' in artistic matters, since I knew they were merely there as watchdogs to oversee the spending of public money and were woefully ignorant about the day to day running of a theatre. I have no reason to believe that John E. Sayers was any more enlightened. His suggestion that Sam's play should be produced in an experimental theatre, 'if such there is in Belfast,' was unrealistic and downright ridiculous. Had he envisaged the pocket-handkerchief stage, the make-shift setting, the cramped auditorium and the large cast (most likely amateur), or any sane producer that might foolishly have undertaken such an enterprise? I think not! 'No, Jack,' I am tempted to say in retrospect. 'Each to his own trade.'

By late September all my commitments to the Group and Bangor had been honoured. Jonathan Goodman, a young man of roughly my own age, had been appointed in my place as artistic director. This would have been in late September or early October and for a short while we shared the same cramped space, he installing himself and getting his bearings and myself clearing up. He appeared to have mainly a television background and was described among other things as a

73

producer of *No Hiding Place*, a popular television series of the time. Under pressure to make an impression, he made several rash statements to the press, one to the effect that the artistic director of a theatre must be 'an absolute dictator,' a remark that could have pleased neither his autocratic chairman nor his company such as it was, (especially coming from an Englishman). Another press release, which proved to be his greatest 'faux pas,' claimed that 'actors were expendable,' a statement that aroused the wrath of all the professional actors in the town. Another remark which I took to be aimed at me earned the headline: "The Group Theatre was advancing backward, says Artistic Director".

I did not have to wait long for my revenge. In a face-to-face confrontation on Independent Television with Mr Goodman I chose my moment, but meanwhile I had done my homework, as the following illustrates:

> "Mr Goodman also revealed, (26 October), that the Group is to put on a new play by Belfast schoolteacher Stewart Love, called 'Randy Dandy' (sic). It was a sort of Ulster *Look Back in Anger* about which he was 'terribly excited'."

Obviously my curiosity was aroused. It was plainly hidden away in a file marked 'New Plays' whilst I had been sharing a desk with the new director. I was, like Jonathan, very impressed with the writing when I sneaked into the theatre to see it, although my admiration did not extend to the young amateur actor who was playing the leading part. On the interview in which Hubert Wilmot of the Arts Theatre acted as a kind of mediator, we fenced politely for a few minutes until I found an opening. 'You have been using a lot of amateurs in your productions, especially in leading parts,' I said. He was very wary as he replied, 'Well there aren't enough professional actors available.' Sensing that he had dropped his guard I went in for the kill. 'Then would you like to publicly withdraw your statement that actors are expendable,' I said. 'I suppose I would have to,' he replied, and I could hear in my head all the actors who had resigned cheering me to the echo; in fact I was to hear later that they had all been glued to their television sets.

But by now the coast was clear and the monthly trips to the board meetings in Dublin went ahead fruitfully and uninterrupted. One diversion was when Henry and myself went to a performance of *West Side Story* in London to see if we could learn something from the staging; we were encountering problems with our 'revolve' and we were considering using 'trucks' to move scenery about on stage. None of these problems were solved by going backstage after the performance but I made a note of the overhead cut-cloths suggesting perspective and drew Henry's attention to them, visualising them also as representing overhead gantries; but that, too, I left to Henry's creative discretion. Henry, I was to discover, was very well connected in London, hence his backstage access and the complimentary tickets to a West End show, plus the fact that our stay in the Piccadilly Hotel was 'on the house' because Henry was redesigning the interiors of that desirable establishment.

In the Eros bar over a late night drink, the problem of the revolve was finally overcome. The difficulty lay in the rectangular design of the revolve itself and the irregular superstructure representing the hull of a ship which surmounted it. As this giant structure with its scaffolding and staging revolved, it would just catch the edge of the proscenium with its third corner. It was then I had a bright idea which I demonstrated to Henry with a cigarette packet: 'What if a second steel bolt were to come into play at this point, aimed at a second socket, drilled and inserted at roughly left of downstage centre?' The cue to remove the centre bolt with a lever would have to be timed perfectly and relayed to a man beneath the stage. Of course we would have to ask permission to drill a second hole and insert a second socket, but I left Henry to sort out all the technical difficulties which he did with his customary flair. Needless to say, we would foot the bill for any repairs.

V

Back in Belfast, J.G. Devlin, who was to take the leading part in *Over The Bridge*, had returned from London and was to play a surprising but not entirely unexpected part in the controversy. Although 'Jimmy' was Northern Ireland's area representative for Equity, the actors' trade union had so far played no public part in the dispute. Now he seized his chance. Hugh Jenkins, the assistant general secretary of British Actors' Equity was coming to Belfast to discuss the Independent Television Authority's requirements from its local stations, which included Ulster Television. A meeting was to be held in the Grand Central Hotel and Jimmy had decided it would be a showdown. He lobbied all the professional actors to attend but did not tell us in advance what he had in mind. To our astonishment, when we got there not only was the room packed, but Mr Ritchie McKee and Mr Harry McMullan were already sitting in the front row in two comfortable seats, but jammed against the wall. Jimmy had escorted them there himself and the rest of the row was packed with actors who had been instructed not to let them out whatever happened, I discovered later. The meeting was reported in the *Belfast Telegraph* of 9th November, but not in full.

Jimmy began his introduction by addressing his remarks to the Government, probably in response to questions asked in the Stormont parliament about the alleged misuse of public money. 'Unless something is done about it there will be no theatre here in six months,' he began, adding that the government apparently, was not satisfied with the present position in the theatre. 'I put it to the government,' he declaimed, 'that the solution to the problem is to get rid of the people now running the Ulster Group Theatre.' 'It seems to me,' he went on, 'that the Group Theatre is being re-launched as an amateur theatre all over again,' adding in stentorian tones and pointing an accusing finger, 'These are the guilty men!' Messrs. McMullan and McKee tried to rise from their seats and make their escape but they were jammed in and had to sit through the rest of the proceedings much to their embarrassment; but for Jimmy it was a triumph and a tour de force.

Hard on the heels of this meeting we organised our first press release, which appeared in the *Belfast Telegraph* of the 12th November along with a photograph of J.G. Devlin, Sam Thompson and myself. It appeared under the heading: Empire to stage play Group banned. And began:

> "Sam Thompson's play *Over The Bridge* is to be presented for a three week season at the Empire Theatre, Belfast, beginning on January 25 ...
>
> "Based on sectarianism and trade unions in the Belfast shipyards, the play was to have been produced by the Group Theatre in May, but was withdrawn by the directors when in rehearsal. Mr Thompson's action for breach of contract was settled out of court.
>
> "J.G. Devlin will play the leading role which was specially written for him – that of a trade union official – and the production will be by James Ellis, formerly director of productions at the Group Theatre. The play will be presented by an independent company.
>
> "Mr Ellis said today: 'I feel that in view of the sorry state of the theatre in Ulster and the situation that arose in connection with *Over The Bridge* it is important that there should be an independent company formed to present plays in Belfast. We will be able to call on a number of professional actors and actresses who are no longer working at the Group but are freelancers. Also, it will be valuable for authors to have more than one market for their plays.'
>
> "'J.G. Devlin has agreed to accept the contract for this presentation even though he is in great demand at present in London for television,' said Mr Ellis. 'Now that we have the principal role cast, we can go ahead with engaging other

actors. The production will not be based on the idea that actors and actresses are expendable. I don't think the Belfast public feel that way about players whose work they have seen and admired over the years.'

"Mr Thompson said: 'I am very glad that the public and the drama critics will get an opportunity of seeing this play for themselves and that it will not be judged by only a few individuals; this will in no sense be a soap-box production,' he commented, adding: 'we are very happy that the play is going on at the Empire and Mr Reynolds, the manager, has been very co-operative in all the negotiations.'"

We were now in the long run-up to the first night, which was not until the New Year, (the 26th January and not the 25th, as the press had reported), but there was still plenty to organise. The first priority was a stable script, which by now had been agreed between Sam and myself, allowing of course for improvisations which would inevitably occur during rehearsals. Henry was present at last minute meetings having read the master-copy before it went to the printers so that he was aware of changing acting areas from 'scene to scene' keeping the action fluid and easy on the eye. Henry reported that the scenery was being constructed by Fitzpatrick & Son, the scaffolding by P.F. Kerr Ltd. Most of the set should be in place by the end of the third week's rehearsal when the Empire stage itself would be free, as Frank Reynolds had not booked any other incoming shows. With a smile he added that Kenneth Jamison, my cousin, was designing a massive front gauze featuring a bridge, worker's houses and shipyard cranes, which would introduce the play.

The casting was not a problem. The actors from the original cast had by and large remained with the Group company while I was still there and resigned, as I had advised them to, only when my provisional agreement to fulfil outstanding obligations had terminated. Now their parts were guaranteed and generous terms were agreed fairly quickly.

I have already said that J.G. Devlin had been much in demand, especially for television roles in London, but he was firmly committed to appearing in *Over The Bridge* and had given me his word on this. Now, typically, he was honouring that commitment and I have to say that at that time a production of *Over The Bridge* would have been unthinkable without him. It is difficult, indeed virtually impossible to describe, the affection in which this most loveable of men was held in the hearts of the public and his fellow actors for whom he had done so much, both collectively and individually. As an actor, his audiences responded to his natural warmth and flawless technique and both in the rehearsal room and on the stage he was a natural leader. There are very few actors of whom this can be said and among the most cherished of my memories are those evoked by Jimmy, both at The Group and across the water, of our appearances on television and with Bill Bryden's Cottesloe Company at the National Theatre. Truly, from the day I met him, we were friends for life.

But to turn the clock back to late 1959, our production was virtually cast. So everything was falling into place; or perhaps not quite. I was worried that Maurice O'Callaghan who had voted with me at the initial meeting, could just possibly be victimised for what the Group's board of directors might regard as an act of treachery. This was a bitter dispute with no holds barred and Maurice, like myself, was a family man, so I advised him to tread warily. Consequently Maurice did not appear in the Belfast production, as we had as yet no clear idea of what might happen at the box office. A young and very talented amateur whose intention at that time was to turn professional, played the part of the victimised Catholic worker in Maurice's place, and played it rather well. It was yet another demonstration that, at least in the Ulster theatre of the time, actors were not expendable and professionals who had not found work in England or elsewhere were comparatively rare.

A notable exception to this was Harry Towb who was living and working in England and was persuaded to return home and take the part of Warren Baxter, the young shop steward. Harry was to be third billing on the posters behind J.G. Devlin and Joseph Tomelty; Harold Goldblatt, my immediate predecessor as artistic director, and founder member of the Group Theatre who had prior engagements, was to join us later; so we had a strong cast, backed by talented supporting players from the wonderful ensemble that had been disrupted by a totally unnecessary dispute.

Joseph Tomelty, previously the general manager and resident playwright of that company had become a film star overnight when in 1951, as a member of Tyrone Guthrie's company, he had been spotted by the powerful London agent, Freddie Joachim. But Joe's celebrity was to come to a sudden and tragic end four years later. On a day off from playing Ava Gardner's father in the film, *Bhowani Junction* he was involved in a horrific car crash and lay in a coma for eleven weeks. He never fully recovered. However, he made several brave attempts to make a comeback to the stage and *Over The Bridge* was one of them. I had directed him in one of his own plays at Bangor but it was a disaster. Nevertheless he still had a warm and endearing stage presence which the part called for and I had decided to take a chance with him. J.G. Devlin would provide the necessary driving force and the young Harry Towb had all his wits about him. They could be relied upon to keep Joe out of trouble and as for the rest of the company, well, he was 'among friends'.

Despite Guthrie's reservations about women being in the play, I had decided to keep them for reasons I have explained earlier. Besides, Joe loved women and they loved him and all three ladies had known and worked with Joe before he became a famous name. Knowing what he had been through, they fussed over him and did everything possible to make him happy; and besides, there were family connections between the characters in the play. Irene Bingham was his devoted wife,

Kathleen Feenan was the beloved daughter and Catherine Gibson was the ambitious wife of his not very supportive brother, George Mitchell. Irene Bingham was unable to leave Belfast for family reasons and was replaced by the inimitable Elizabeth Begley. But the consistently excellent Catherine Gibson and Kathleen Feenan, who, as Marion Mitchell, was engaged to the young shop steward, Warren Mitchell, was, as she had been in *When We are Married*, simply outstanding. All three ladies travelled to Dublin and remained with the tour and its subsequent appearance in the West End.

I have little recollection now of the rehearsals apart from the fact that for the first three weeks they were held in the large downstairs room of our then family home at 12 Mount Charles. The setting was a drama in itself. Our little daughter, Amanda was wandering in and out of the room in wonderment at what was going on, while upstairs her mother Betty was giving birth to a baby brother, christened Adam James, tragically to be murdered twenty eight years and seven months later in London. However, all that was far in the future and I have mainly my second wife Robina to thank for drawing a grieving family together in a way that at one time might have seemed impossible after what was an acrimonious divorce for which, incidentally she was in no way responsible. Back in Mount Charles, half a century ago, my little daughter stole the limelight by peeping round the door and having her picture taken by an eagle-eyed newspaper reporter.

My customary modus operandi for the early days of rehearsal, picked up from Guthrie, was to arrange the entrances and exits and only loosely to visualise groupings and confrontations, leaving room for changes and fluidity of movement and allowing scope and latitude for the initiative of individual actors, which in J.G. Devlin's case often involved a good deal of latitude. Only when things began to take shape or were going woefully wrong did I intervene, using my powers of persuasion rather than rigid preconceptions to get roughly my own way. The pace and flow of the dialogue was another matter, and this would emerge only when the actors were fluent with their lines and were securely 'off the book'. Joe Tomelty struggled most in this department and the prompter was alerted to come in quickly with his cues. The other priority was that since Sam had written strongly defined characters with distinct personalities, it was vital that a generalised 'shipyard worker's persona' did not blur this important distinction.

With Henry's scaffolding and staging due to arrive, it was inevitable that I should already have envisaged men in groups both on and above stage level observing the action below or at some remove, as often as not with cynical disregard, but sometimes with dangerously aroused sectarian virulence or amused detachment as the scene demanded. They would be in effect, a sort of 'Greek Chorus' of shipyard workers; and as luck would have it, I had just the men for the job.

The Lord Carson Memorial Flute Band had been used the previous year in Tyrone Guthrie's production of *The Bonefire* and if my memory serves me right he had arranged for them to travel to Edinburgh for the festival. Now I had persuaded them to join the *Over The Bridge* company; and what an asset they proved to be. When their voices were raised individually or collectively, it was the authentic sound of the docklands; but sadly they were to prove irreplaceable when we moved away from Belfast and neither they nor we could afford for them to travel. I cannot now remember when they were introduced to the cast but I recall that we gave them a reading of the play at the end of a day's rehearsal and then retired to the Kitchen Bar to celebrate. It was then I identified the man who had been singled out by Guthrie to lead the entire ensemble and deliver a line that was projected to the back of the theatre. I decided he was the man to do the same job for me and already had in mind an improvised line that was not in the script. It was a saying of my uncle John, himself a shipyard riveter, who after a disappointing boxing match was wont to say disdainfully: 'There's neither of the two of them could bate their way out of a paper bag!' I had offered the line to Sam and when my man from the Lord Carson Band delivered that line in the theatre, he literally brought the house down.

VI

I cannot adequately put into words the excitement and euphoria of that opening night, which took place on the 26th January, 1960. Both before and after, and needless to say during the performance, when the adrenalin was in full flow, we sensed the sweet smell of success; and to Sam in particular, all the confrontations and sacrifices, all the frustrations and postponements, must now have seemed worthwhile; it was after all nearly nine months since his play had been unceremoniously withdrawn. I believed at the time and still think so today, that it was the most sensational as well as the most outspoken play ever to be staged in Belfast and that Sam Thompson's voice was the authentic voice of the shipyard; to attempt to silence that voice was in my view nothing short of a crime. Had I not thought so I doubt if I would have put my job on the line, a decision that was to change my life.

Nearly half a century later the actor Harry Towb, then, like myself, one of the few survivors of that production, said that his reaction when he first read the play was that it could never be put on in Belfast. He also thought that I was taking 'a tremendous chance' and showing 'immense courage' in daring to stage it; but 'fair play to him,' he added, 'he put it on.' And, may I say, 'fair play to Harry,' who has sadly since died. He accepted the part of the young shop steward and returned to his native Northern Ireland. He described the theatre on the opening night as 'surrounded by policemen and B Specials with revolvers on the hip and at the ready,' which I think was a bit of an exaggeration, but certainly there was a significant police presence, and guns on prominent display were customary at that time in what is often mistakenly referred to as 'The Province'. The audience however, from

83

gallery to circle and stalls, was agog with excitement and anticipation but exceedingly good-natured and well behaved. There were queues at the box office and even longer queues for the gallery well before curtain up time. Sam found my own father standing in the gallery queue and confronted me angrily backstage; he of course knew my father and had heard his opinion of the play. 'What sort of a son are you,' he growled, 'letting his father queue for the gods?' 'I have two complimentary seats for my mother and father booked in the front stalls,' I yelled back, 'but he said they didn't want to get in the way on our opening night.' Sam smoothed the way by grabbing the old man, escorting him to his seat and giving him a programme; and what a night he had, joining in the celebrations backstage, meeting the cast and going home in a taxi.

Once and for all, I would like to put paid to all the persistent rumours that the after the show party was held at George and Mercy McCann's flat in Botanic Avenue where the poet Louis McNeice was staying. This is apparently recorded in Sam Hanna Bell's journals; but as far as I am aware these are not, and never were in general circulation; they seem to be private family papers. However, to be realistic, apart from the fact that the McCann's flat – and I was there on many occasions – was far too small to host such an event, there was no way that either Sam or myself would have deserted our loyal cast at such a time. Everyone was invited, including the entire stage staff, the front of house staff and, not least, the entire Lord Carson Memorial Flute Band who had performed outstandingly. I can only put the rumours down to name dropping, snobbery, or sheer guesswork; it was, and still is, I believe, just another example of everyone trying to get in on the act.

As for memories of the actual performance, or instructions beforehand, there was too much mayhem going on to leave time for any of that. I was, for example, unable to hide behind a curtain in one of the boxes – they were all packed – and the back of the stalls was likewise packed with standing room only ticket-holders. Consequently I was unable to watch any of the first half from the front of house and had to content myself with a very limited view from the wings where I was constantly getting in the way. I could sense, however that the adrenalin was flowing freely and that the entire cast were in top form. I also watched with admiration as stage manager Herbert Stilling and his staff, supervised by Henry Lynch Robinson, coped with every problem. The great 'Double Revolve', for example, turned triumphantly without a hitch – horns and whistles blowing, with an accompaniment of cheers to evoke the launching of a ship – and this in turn was greeted by loud applause and more cheers from an audience largely made up of shipyard workers. Anticipating this, Henry and I had chosen this moment to impress our audience with this display of technology and it certainly had the desired effect. Sam, of course, was onstage playing the part of Archie Kerr, so he must have experienced at first hand, after all our trials and tribulations, that his play was well on its way to silencing his detractors and critics. I too, at this point, sensed that we had a triumph on our hands and knowing we had a powerful second half to come, went confidently backstage to prepare for my entrance as the mob leader.

The play's reception was tumultuous and it took several minutes for the applause to die down. When it did, I made the mistake of stepping forward to introduce Sam, but when I opened my mouth to speak, a voice from the gallery yelled: 'We don't want to hear you, we want to hear Sam!' Knowing I was beaten, I backed off but not before yelling back in my still strong East Belfast accent: 'If you'll shut your mouth for just a minute that's what I'm here to do,' quickly announcing: 'Ladies and gentlemen, Mr Sam Thompson.' Sam waited for me to acknowledge a sympathetic burst of applause before stepping forward to a resounding cheer.

That defining moment demonstrated beyond all doubt that literally overnight, Sam Thompson had become a folk hero and the shipyard man's champion; but beyond that, it proved that the Belfast public preferred to be the judge of what it chose to see rather than have that choice made for them.

It is worth noting the young Alex Findlater's memories of the occasion as recorded in his book of 2001, and his first hand response to the controversy:

> "On the opening night, 26 January 1960, the tension was immense. The RUC were thick in Victoria Square and the streets around the Empire. There was an expectation that there would be trouble but none materialised. The theatre was packed to capacity and the audience responded to the powerful plot and outstanding performances. Dermot, his wife Dorothea, John McGrail, Frank Reynolds and Jimmy Ellis, all directors, must have shared a great sense of elation as the evening concluded successfully without incident. And to top it all, the reviews were excellent …"

He also wrote elsewhere in the book:

> "Jimmy Ellis must take the credit for seeing that this important play was staged. He was at that time producer director at the Group Theatre. He felt very strongly that it should be staged, and without cuts. He resigned over the issue and formed a new company to make certain that Belfast should see it.' 'We are not afraid of this play' he said. 'It is honest and should be judged by that standard.'"

After all these years it is refreshing to read such an accurate and impartial summary of the occasion, though at the time no one in Belfast suspected that I was a director of Findlater & Company as well as of Ulster Bridge Productions. It was all part and parcel of our 'cloak and dagger' operation. In the event a hurried meeting of both sets of directors was called for the following day when it was decided to extend our estimated run from three to six weeks and to discuss the distinct possibility of a Dublin run. From then on it was important to keep in touch with our Dublin partners through myself and Frank Reynolds.

One pleasant and totally unexpected surprise of the first week was an enquiry from His Excellency the Governor of Northern Ireland. His equerry rang to say that His Excellency regretted he could not attend the opening night in an official capacity, but wondered if we could arrange two seats for himself and Lady Wakehurst in a prominent position in the stalls for the Saturday night. Oh, and one thing more, Lord and Lady Wakehurst would very much like to meet the author and the cast after the show and perhaps stay for a drink. My excitement knew no bounds, and of course I re-arranged the seating to accommodate their Excellencies before rushing off to tell Sam and Henry, (Frank was in the office with me). Then it occurred to me that this was probably Henry's doing, for he had friends in high places and most likely had hatched the plot with the equerry himself or one of his aides; but he said nothing, just raised an eyebrow. 'What would Ritchie McKee have to say,' I thought, 'if the news got back to him.' Sam, needless to say, was over the moon about meeting the Governor. In spite of being a member of the Labour Party, he had a keen understanding of publicity and knew this would be another one in the eye for our adversaries. As he remarked to me with a shrug and a grin, 'these 'royals' are above politics.'

Lord Wakehurst was wonderfully indiscreet after the performance and in congratulating the author and cast he said quite openly that he didn't understand what all the fuss was about. 'Why did they take it upon themselves to ban this play?' he demanded, and he was to elaborate on this theme in the stalls bar where we had laid on something of a party. As the drinks flowed certain members of his entourage tried to drag him away, and even Lady Wakehurst was looking a little apprehensive, but the Governor was enjoying himself and was not to be budged. Sam and he got on famously and were soon swapping stories. Inevitably of course Ritchie McKee's name cropped up and His

Excellency remarked coolly: 'Yes I have met Mr McKee, I think.' Finally the evening came to an end and a good time was had by all, but there is an amusing coda to the Governor's visit and this story I had, as they say, from a very reliable source. Shortly after the visit, Lord Wakehurst and Mr McKee just happened to be attending the same official function, and as he was leaving he spotted him and called out: 'Any riots yet McKee?'

Perhaps now is the time to give my impressions of the general culture of the time as I remember it and explain as well as I can Mr McKee's paranoia and apparent thirst for power together with his position, or positions, as a watchdog for the establishment. I have already mentioned his instincts as a natural courtier and the powerful positions he held in the fields of the arts and broadcasting; the fact that he was the prime minister's habitual golfing partner is likewise not entirely irrelevant. A golf course is at once a private and confidential setting to discuss matters of state. The points I will raise include subjects I discussed with the late Paddy Devlin which he later published in the magazine *Theatre Ireland* but the views that follow are entirely the result of my own conclusions and observations.

The then Governor of Northern Ireland and the Queen's representative, Lord Wakehurst, was of a liberal, not to say cavalier turn of mind, as epitomised in his attendance, albeit as a private individual, at Sam Thompson's play, an independent gesture to say the least. The Unionist establishment, however, under Lord Brookeborough (then, I believe, Sir Basil Brooke), was far from liberal. As always, but under his leadership more especially so, it was determined to hold onto power at any price and silence all voices of protest or dissent, real or imagined. The paranoia came from the very top and was manifest in the persona of Ritchie McKee. Paddy Devlin thought, and I am inclined to believe him, that Sir Basil subtly used his influence to manoeuvre McKee into key positions, especially in theatre and broadcasting, (both means of communication not unknown to totalitarian regimes), in order to monitor unacceptable trends and opinions. Now I am aware that this is a bit of an exaggeration and I know that the Republic of Ireland exercised sweeping powers of censorship through the Church with its notorious index and that as well as books, plays were also banned, driving Sean O'Casey out of the country; James Joyce had already left in 1904.

Before *Over The Bridge*, the principal exercise of political pressure had been employed frequently it must be said, through the BBC as the regional governor and his head of programmes attempted to put pressure on the national network to censor completely or alter to their satisfaction certain transmissions concerning what was referred to as 'The Province'. Very few of these programmes justified their actions and they were in grave danger of making themselves a laughing stock, though I doubt if Sir Basil thought so. He had not moved the proverbial 'one inch' from the dictum of the first prime minister of Northern Ireland, Lord Craigavon, who called his government, with twelve seats in Westminster, 'A Protestant Parliament for a Protestant People'. That was hardly a recipe for democracy with its slogan 'Government of the People, by the People and for the People'.

That such a state of affairs could not last forever was not apparent at the time, but perhaps Sam Thompson, drawing on past experience, instinctively knew that the destructive power of sectarianism, especially if it was linked to violent or militant action, could bring the body politic to its knees. I must emphasise however that *Over The Bridge* conveys no hint of this and is, in Sam's own words 'a plea for tolerance'. A more pertinent word of warning is unequivocally conveyed in a speech by the great Irish orator and statesman, Edmund Burke, when he says that 'a state without the means of some change is without the means of its conservation.' To whom it may concern, I would humbly draw attention to some other wise words of Burke which are that 'Politics and the pulpit are terms that have little agreement.'

The weeks that followed were certainly exciting and I cannot now remember in what particular order events occurred, but certainly news of something spectacular happening in the theatre in Belfast quickly spread. Louis MacNeice had reviewed the play favourably for the *Guardian* I think, and *The Critics*, an up-market programme on BBC radio, had hailed the production as a triumph, comparing me to Tyrone Guthrie as an up and coming young director. For whatever reason, Sam's controversial play and the huge audiences it was attracting drew interested parties like a magnet. First on the doorstep was a man called Granger, later to become a producer of *Coronation Street*: he must have attended the opening night and rang up the following day to make an appointment. He offered £2,000 for the rights to produce the play on Granada Television, an offer which we accepted. Then Robert Kemp, who was in charge of appointing an artistic director for a newly formed Scottish National Theatre at the Gateway in Edinburgh offered me the job, but of course it was out of the question with my urgent commitments and my loyalties to Sam and the company. Nevertheless, at a much later date when the offer was still open, I travelled to Edinburgh at Mr Kemp's pressing invitation and was shown around the theatre which was to be home to the national company and was informed that the job was still open. The first play to be presented would be the Norwegian dramatist Bjornson's tragic drama *Mary Stuart in Scotland* and it would be staged in the grand manner. It was a tempting prospect but again I had no option but to remain loyal to Ulster Bridge Productions. To this day, I am keenly aware of the irony that at the time I was being rejected by the powers that be in my own community, I was being pressed to accept a similar position, with no strings attached, in a country across the water with a not dissimilar culture from our own. I was never again to be offered such a prestigious post, either in Ireland or elsewhere and, though I didn't know it at the time, my future would be as an actor.

As for *Over The Bridge*, the next move came from us. We had already been approached by Laurence Olivier Productions (LOP) through his director, Laurier Lister who had seen the play praised by an enthusiastic Belfast public and press and had reported back to the great man himself.

To arouse the interest of such a renowned figure was unheard of. No play from Northern Ireland had ever transferred across the water unless you count Tyrone Guthrie's Festival Company, formed especially for the occasion. However, this time, after a short tour, we were to appear, in association with Laurence Olivier Productions, in London's West End. Of course Sam and I were over the moon at the prospect, as was Henry and the entire cast, but neither Olivier himself, nor Laurier Lister, took any part in the production; it was accepted as a proven success and in fact Olivier never saw it. He had intended to fly over to Dublin to see it but was prevented from doing so by an Aer Lingus strike. The only appointment made by LOP was the company manager and stage director, David Cross.

Now is as good a time as any to mention that *Over The Bridge* was not in fact the first play to be written by a Belfast man who also happened to be a shipyard worker. It was called *Workers* and it was by Thomas Carnduff. It was produced by the Abbey Theatre in Dublin and received mixed reviews. One example, quoted by the Belfast historian, Dr. Jonathan Bardon is from the *Irish Times* whose critique concludes with the sentence: 'For an out of work shipyard employee who had no previous experience of the stage, it is a remarkable achievement.' It was staged in 1932, but sadly, people have short memories. *Workers* was Carnduff's first play, but his other work was produced by The Belfast Repertory Company whose home in the 1930s was, ironically, The Empire Theatre.

However to return to our immediate concerns. It was understood that the West End production of *Over The Bridge* would have to be put on hold until we had maximised our returns in Ireland, both in the North and in the South. As well as estimating the run in Belfast – a difficult enough problem as we were to discover to our cost – there was a huge demand for tickets at the end of the run but by then the die had been cast and I had made our arrangements with a Dublin theatre. In fact, despite some apprehensions, due I believe to inexperience, Dublin had turned out to be no big deal, as I will now endeavour to relate.

We already had a hint from an unconfirmed press report that the Dublin management of Ilsley and McCabe had been sniffing around Belfast in search of a venue for their own production but that was now clearly out of the question. Then I had tentative enquiries not only from them, but also from Louis Elliman, the proprietor of the Gaiety Theatre. It was my cue to travel south and I made arrangements to see Mr Elliman in the morning and Messrs Ilsley and McCabe early in the afternoon. It was my first experience of negotiating a deal and though I was wary, in particular of Mr Elliman, I told myself that we were negotiating from strength and decided to play it by ear.

Louis Elliman was the most powerful figure in Dublin theatre at that time and here was I, a rookie 'entrepreneur', facing across a desk, a man with a big cigar trying to negotiate a deal for the fledgling company, Ulster Bridge Productions. I decided to let him do the talking. 'You will have Orson Welles preceding you with his production of *Chimes at Midnight*.' This was, I think, meant to impress me which of course it did, but I made no reply as Mr Elliman continued blithely: 'Like everything else in the theatre this is an unknown quantity so you might have to postpone your Dublin visit, but from what I hear, your production might extend to another week, or even two?' This last suggestion had been put in the form of a query and I began to stammer: 'B-but we've already extended the run for an extra three weeks,' I said. Unfazed by any of this he got down to discussing terms. 'Now I know you have been a huge success in Belfast but there is no guarantee of the same thing happening in Dublin,' he said. 'I am also aware that it is an expensive production and for that reason I'm prepared to offer you fifty five percent of the gross box office takings leaving us with

92

forty five percent; there will be no guarantee against loss.' Then he added by way of dismissal, 'that is my final offer.' I rose from my seat to thank him for his time and after shaking hands I found myself saying: 'I'll let you know when I've reported back to my fellow directors; in the meantime I have some other people to see.' I could tell he knew I was on my way to see his arch rivals Ilsley and McCabe so I made my exit fairly swiftly and found my way to Neary's bar for a spot of lunch before heading for Dame Street and the Olympia Theatre.

Stanley Ilsley and Leo McCabe were a different kettle of fish entirely from Mr Louis Elliman. Sheer theatrical camp, they inhabited a flat above their theatre that was pure kitch and ornamented with gaudy properties and memorabilia from their own productions including the skull from Stanley's Hamlet and a not very good full-length portrait of himself in that role. They poured me a sherry, perhaps to soften me up, and then we got down to business, or 'show business,' as Stanley remarked airily. I told them straight away that I had been to see Louis Elliman that morning and Leo remarked that he was a tough nut to crack, or words to that effect; but I assured them that he had offered extremely good terms. 'Well that's a turn up for the books,' said Leo in an almost surly manner, as though he had been thrown onto the back foot. I came straight to the point: 'Mr Elliman has offered us fifty five percent of the gross takings because it is obviously an expensive production,' I said, 'and you will have to do better than that, because in all honesty I would have to go back to him if he were to be the highest bidder.'

'We can match that,' said Leo in desperation, 'and ours is by far the larger theatre.'

'That's not the point,' I replied, 'it would have to be sixty/forty, in our favour. I don't know how long a pause there was but it lasted for some time before the silence was broken by Stanley offering a sherry and saying with a distinct upward inflexion: 'Agreed Leo?'

'I suppose we have no option,' said Leo.

After ringing Dermot Findlater to pass on the good news, I hastened back to Belfast with the contract signed and sealed. Needless to say, Sam and Henry were delighted with the terms, 'you couldn't possibly have got that deal from Louis Elliman,' said Henry, so I told them the whole story of my trip, underlining the fact that we had secured the larger of the two theatres, which Henry thought was the better venue for our virtually epic production. Then an awful thought struck me: 'How would we fare without the Lord Carson Memorial Flute Band?' It was only the first of many problems that would crop up on the way but it had to be faced. I rang Dermot Doolan at Irish Equity and asked if there were any extras available in a few weeks' time. He laughed at the very idea, saying that Ardmore Film Studios was in full production and employing every available extra; but he had a helpful suggestion to make. Why didn't I phone a colonel, (and he gave me his name), at Phoenix Park barracks and ask for a platoon of the Irish army; he was sure he would oblige. This, strangely enough, turned out to be the solution to the problem, with amusing though highly professional consequences.

A week or so later another mildly amusing phone call asking for me occurred. When I responded the caller announced herself as Orson Welles's secretary. She wondered if I could confirm the date for the opening of our play in Dublin and I obliged. Now I knew that if Sam was a fan of any film star it was Orson Welles and his all-time favourite film was *Citizen Kane*, so when Sam walked into the theatre that evening I called out: 'You're famous Sam. Orson Welles wants to know what date your play is opening in Dublin.' Privately I envisaged Mr Elliman and Orson in the office at the Gaiety Theatre wondering how best to go about asking that question without losing face. By now news would have spread on the theatrical grapevine that Sam's play was a record-breaking phenomenon so they must have wondered if losing control of it to a rival theatre wasn't a tactical error.

Some time during the Dublin run we had acquired the services of a top London agent to represent us which I remember was London Management. As a consequence, I was making regular trips to the metropolis while my understudy stood in for me and on one of those trips I was taken out to lunch in Wheeler's of Old Compton Street by William McQuitty, the producer of the first Titanic film, *A Night to Remember*. McQuitty was a canny Ulsterman and we got along just fine but after a Dover sole and a couple of bottles of Grand Cru Chablis he offered me £1,000 for provisional rights to *Over The Bridge*. I told him that neither Sam, nor our agents, would accept such an offer and that we preferred to gamble on the success of the play in London. I added that *The Summer of the Seventeenth Doll*, another Olivier production, after its successful London run, had been bought by the American movie moguls Hecht, Hill, Lancaster, for a sum well in excess of half a million pounds. 'After it was a proven stage success,' he replied. 'I'm making my offer before it has proved itself and I'm sure we could insert a clause to allow for adjusting that offer.' 'But Granada Television has already bought the rights to televise the play for £2,000' I said, and on that note I thanked him for the lunch and we parted company. Many years later I met William McQuitty at an exhibition in the Tate Gallery and he said I had made a mistake in turning down his offer. He had seen the play in Belfast where it was at its best and that is where he would have made his film. I shall never know the truth.

We were forced to open in Dublin though we were still playing to full houses in Belfast, because we had committed ourselves and there was no turning back. Well over forty thousand people had seen the play over a six week period; some reports say five weeks but I trust my own memory. The fact is that the people of Belfast had voted with their feet, completely justifying our protest against interference by the establishment. Perhaps, more significantly, many of those who came had never set foot in a theatre before. However, above all, I believe that our stand cleared the way for future playwrights and producers and never again would the kind of busybodies we had to deal with dare to interfere in the artistic affairs of the theatre, not even at the height of 'The Troubles'.

In Dublin everything went according to plan; well almost. The main thing was that the demand for tickets for the opening night was enormous and the advance bookings at the box office were beyond all expectations. The one snag at this stage came from Leo McCabe himself. He was appalled at the idea of a second hole being drilled in his stage despite the fact that he had been shown the entire operation of the revolve on a visit to Belfast. Now he claimed that his entire stage would have to be re-floored and I suspected that perhaps he was trying to recoup some of the loss he was incurring by the terms of our agreement. Whatever the case, pacing to the right of centre stage he pointed to a spot where dry rot or woodworm had done its work and a hole had gone right through the boards.

'What's that?' I enquired.

'That was the leg of Semprini's piano; it went clean through' he replied, somewhat flustered. 'You see my stage won't stand heavy weights,' he added.

Semprini was a famous concert pianist of the time who had chosen the variety stage as the easiest way to earn good money, but I still couldn't fathom what Leo McCabe was driving at.

'What are you expecting me to do about it?' I asked.

'Well my stage will not stand up to the heavy scenery you are bringing in, so I'm expecting you to re-floor it.'

'Well I'm not paying for the damage done by the leg of Semprini's piano,' I said, pacing to centre stage. 'If you want the whole thing re-floored I'll pay for my half,' and I borrowed a piece of chalk from a stagehand and drew a dividing line right down the middle. Fortunately, the 'get in' wasn't for a couple of days and work, which went on through the night, started immediately, so we weren't seriously delayed. When I told Henry the story on his arrival he was much amused but said it was probably just as well, since half rotten boards might well have given way under the strain, with disastrous consequences.

Another crisis that arose during the first week was an attempted unofficial strike by the stage hands who moved scenery in full view of the audience, wearing dungarees provided by the visiting company. One morning in midweek, before setting up for the evening performance, one of the younger members of the crew, supported vocally by a colleague of roughly the same age, announced belligerently that there would be no performance on the Saturday night unless their money was quadrupled. I asked him if he was the shop steward and a voice from above, (the electrician who did not qualify for appearance money), called down in a broad Dublin brogue: 'Nuttin' to do with me!' So I called up to the electrician: 'Are you the shop steward?' And the voice came down as before: 'Nuttin' to do with me!' 'It might have nothin' to do with him,' said the belligerent one, 'but it has everythin' to do with us! We're the ones who have to appear.'

Thinking on my feet, I knew I had to take swift action, so I said in what I hoped were conciliatory tones: 'Your headquarters are in Merrion Square aren't they?' I knew perfectly well what the address was but I wanted to take the initiative. 'That's right, sir,' they said, a little less belligerently, and I knew I was getting the upper hand. 'I tell you what,' I went on, 'why don't I get a taxi and we'll go round there.' It was the head office of the powerful Irish Transport and General Workers' Union and we met without delay the General Secretary, Mr Frank Robbins who immediately wanted to know what the problem was, so I told him. 'These lads are looking for a pay rise well above the minimum and I've already checked what that is,' I said. 'It's a stage play we are doing at the Olympia Theatre called *Over The Bridge* and the stagehands are required to change the scenery in full view of the audience but there is no acting required; a platoon of the Irish Army are taking care of that since Irish Equity's members are fully employed at Ardmore.' Frank seemed amused by this but questioned the two lads

97

further. 'Don't you have a shop steward to deal with these matters?' he asked. 'He said it was nothin' to do with him,' said the belligerent one. 'Would you just wait outside for a few minutes,' said Frank. I knew it was all over, but Frank Robbins was most apologetic. I explained that the author, Sam Thompson and myself were strong trade unionists and fully intended to give the stagehands, including the electrician, a handsome bonus at the end of the run. 'You'll have nothing further to worry about, Jimmy,' he said, before calling the lads back in and giving them a fatherly dressing down. He also presented me with a signed copy of *Fifty Years of Liberty Hall – The Golden Jubilee of the Irish Transport and General Workers' Union 1909-1959*. It was later inscribed by the book's editor, Cathal O'Shannon:

> To Jimmy Ellis, in appreciation of his fine production of Sam Thompson's *Over The Bridge* in the Olympia Theatre … April 10th, 1960.

That inscription, with its historic signature, means more to me than all the critical reviews and I have kept that book as a treasured memento of one of the most thrilling episodes of my life.

The rehearsals with the Irish army turned out to be an exhilarating as well as an amusing part of the Dublin production. It was certainly then, and still is, a unique element in my theatrical experience. At ten o'clock sharp they were marched onto the newly built stage by their sergeant major and on the call of 'company halt' came to a stop at exactly centre stage and faced front standing rigidly to attention until the order came to 'stand at ease'. Somewhat embarrassed, I thanked the sergeant major for their splendid entrance, muttering something about there being no need to do this performance on every occasion, but he hadn't finished: 'Now you will listen carefully to what the director has to say and carry out his instructions to the letter,' he bellowed, then after a shake of hands he said: 'Over to you sir.'

I soon put them, and myself, at ease and found them the most friendly and willing bunch of fellows, prepared to try anything. What they lost in not having the authentic Belfast accent they made up for in sheer energy and discipline. They picked up the idea of the 'Greek Chorus' of onlookers and formed themselves into natural groups watching the action develop. I even found one likely lad to deliver the line about fighting their way out of a paper bag with a very creditable northern accent; this miracle I achieved by asking for volunteers and I had more than one taker, much to everybody's amusement. This exercise even helped to develop the collective shipyard workers' voice and I brought Sam into the picture at some stage to demonstrate the real thing; as well as myself of course as another genuine East Ender. We were much amused to hear them trying it out during the tea breaks and at other times, but it was when we rehearsed the mob scene of course, that these excellent young men came into their own. I had them climbing the scaffolding and fighting high above the stage. I even remember one young man performing a stunt that involved falling onto a mattress as though into the water, a feat that in itself drew a round of applause from the audience every night; naturally enough we had concealed the mattress behind a piece of scenery. All in all the Irish Army served us well and we did not miss our friends in the Lord Carson Memorial Flute Band too much.

The opening night was a typical Dublin theatrical occasion, packed to the roof with VIPs from every walk of life, including as I remember, Siobhán McKenna, Anew McMaster and Lord Kilannan who was to become a sort of patron of Sam lending him a house on his estate of Spiddal in County Galway to finish his next play. Overnight Sam was to become a celebrity in Dublin as he already was in Belfast and he loved every minute of it. At a press conference the following morning held in the old Dolphin Hotel at the back of the theatre, Sam announced proudly that he was having luncheon with Lord Kilannan and daring to prompt him I tugged his sleeve and suggested 'lunch', but Sam, in full flow, rounded on me and said, 'Lord Kilannan doesn't have his lunch, he takes his luncheon!'

I remember meeting the elderly Anew McMaster in a corridor on that opening night, and after graciously introducing himself he complimented me on the production. McMaster was one of my heroes of the Irish theatre and his compliment that night was my moment of glory. I had seen him play Hamlet at the age of over sixty and it was my turn to compliment him on a fine performance and a truly remarkable career. My memory of the rest of that spectacular evening when we knew for certain that we had conquered the knowledgeable and highly critical Dublin audience, is simply a blur.

Sam's next obsession was to meet Orson Welles and he discovered that *Chimes at Midnight* had a different matinée day to our own so he suggested we book seats to go and see it. Somehow I felt uncomfortable about this because I was sure Welles would be unhappy that we had stolen his limelight. My worst fears were confirmed when we got to the Gaiety Theatre and found it not just half full but virtually empty. We sat through a lack-lustre performance with a not very good supporting cast and worse still, Sam insisted on going to the stage door to introduce himself and asked to meet Orson. Needless to say, his request to meet the great man was rejected and we were turned away.

There was, however, a sequel to this episode. It was to be the last week of *Chimes at Midnight* and *Over The Bridge* had literally driven Orson Welles out of Dublin, as we were to discover; but that was not quite the end of the story, as the following rather ugly incident will illustrate. Usually our cast retired to the big lounge bar of The Dolphin Hotel (sadly no longer there), where a welcoming night porter and a big log fire were awaiting us, but just once in a while, especially on a Saturday night, some of us would pay a visit to Alfredo's night club which happened to serve a good late night meal. That very Saturday Sam, myself and a few members of the cast decided on a treat to mark the end of our first week in Dublin. When we arrived we found that we were sitting at a table just a few feet away from Orson Welles, who had his back to us. He had booked a very large table and his entire cast were gathered round it, along with his director, Hilton Edwards, because it was their closing night. Hilton was sitting sideways on so Sam was able to catch his eye; he beckoned him over. I had not realised that Sam had met him at his own opening night but apparently this was so:

'Introduce me to Orson,' said Sam imperiously.

Hilton looked apprehensive as he replied nervously, 'Orson's just telling a story.'

'That's all right I'll wait,' said Sam.

After what seemed like an eternity Hilton rose from his seat and swept past us without a word, but apparently he was going to the toilet. Sam's frustration was apparent and his anger was mounting, but his fury knew no bounds when Hilton Edwards ignored him on the way back. Sam stuck out a hand and held Hilton's in a vice-like grip. What followed was an unstoppable flow of invective and insults, many of them to do with Hilton's sexual proclivities. It was certainly embarrassing, but when I say unstoppable, it only came to an end when Orson Welles rose from his seat and advanced towards Sam roaring, 'Who is this bum insulting Hilton?' Both Sam and I were on our feet in a trice, but now it was Orson who was unstoppable. He advanced on Sam with his huge bulk and sensing a punch-up I endeavoured to get between them, but it ended in no more than a battle of stomachs as the megastar propelled Sam and myself across the small dance floor and against the far wall of the nightspot. Satisfied that he had won the day he stormed out with Hilton in tow, though his actors to a man, (and woman), remained behind. So celebrated was our hitherto unknown Belfast playwright and so intrigued were Welles' actors to meet Sam, that they gathered around and hung on his every word. Sadly that was Sam's one and only chance to meet his idol, though he did 'confront him' after a fashion. Strangely enough, Orson Welles attended the opening night of *Over The Bridge* in London's West End though needless to say he did not come backstage to meet the author.

Early in the Dublin run, the arrangements with Laurence Olivier Productions were firmly in place and the projected plan was to undertake a fairly short tour of the King's Theatre Glasgow, the Lyceum, Edinburgh and the Theatre Royal, Brighton, before opening in the West End in a theatre that had not yet been decided upon; but that was the way, we were to understand, with London theatres. They were always subject to last-minute availability and it was very much down to the luck of the draw whether or not you got a favourable venue for your particular production. In the meantime I was to-ing and fro-ing to our London agents quite often, keeping my understudy fairly busy. I was familiar with the Lyceum, Edinburgh from the Guthrie production of *The Bonefire* but I decided to pay a visit to the King's, Glasgow to check it out. It was around this time I met David Cross, Laurier Lister's man who was to be our stage director for the entire run.

Over The Bridge was, not surprisingly, a success in Glasgow though not up to the record-breaking standards of Belfast and Dublin. More surprisingly perhaps it also went down well in Edinburgh and, most surprisingly of all, it had a terrific success in Brighton, which was thought to be the best venue to evaluate a potential London success. Naturally we were buoyed up with much optimism and could barely wait for our London opening.

A West End theatre had at last been found. It was the old Prince's Theatre, (since renamed the Shaftesbury), and by now it had been established that David Cross would rehearse the extras, an arrangement that I was not entirely happy with. As I entered the building to supervise what was going on, my heart sank. The building itself was a great barn of a place, which in itself was not too alarming, but gathered on the huge stage was the most lack-lustre bunch of extras imaginable. Most of them were middle-aged if not downright elderly and the collective 'drone' emanating from these clapped out old cronies was pure or rather impure cockney. My heart sank. Was this the shape of things to come? The stage hands didn't seem much better and I seriously began to wonder if they were up to the job. David tried to reassure me by saying that it was 'early days,' but after having a go at trying to inject some life into them I retired to a nearby bar for a sandwich and a drink where I met some gloomy looking characters who were apparently licking their wounds. When they discovered that I had just come from the theatre where we were in the actual process of 'getting in' they introduced themselves and offered their sympathies. One of them was Jimmy Gilbert, soon to become BBC's Head of Comedy who had written the book for a musical called *The Golden Something* and another was Peter Powell, the author of a musical drama called *Johnny the Priest*. *The Golden Something* had come off in a matter of days and *Johnny the Priest* had lasted for exactly a fortnight. This was all the more surprising since it had a very strong cast including Jeremy Brett, Bunny May and Stephanie Voss, but my new-found friends explained that our theatre had become known as 'the graveyard of plays' and they racked their brains for reasons why it had gained this reputation: firstly, it was on the fringe of theatreland, secondly it was isolated on a traffic island and thirdly, once word has got around, a fickle public was liable to take its favours elsewhere. Certainly, I thought to myself, the omens were not good.

Despite my misgivings, which I was at pains not to transmit to Sam or the cast, it is impossible to describe the excitement and anticipation that led up to that opening night. A premiere in the West End is extra special and is something that I personally had not experienced before. Needless to say, I was at one and the same time a nervous wreck and, paradoxically, on cloud nine. The first nights in Belfast and Dublin had both been triumphs but this glamorous occasion under the aegis of Laurence Olivier seemed to me to be the culmination of all our efforts since that fateful day when Sam's play was 'withdrawn from production'.

I spoke to Sam, J.G. Devlin, Joe Tomelty and all the other members of the cast to wish them luck in the usual way, before hiding in a vacant box to watch the performance until I made my appearance as the mob leader later in the play. I did not have time to check who the VIP's were on Laurence Olivier's guest list, but we received a telegram from 'Larry' wishing us all luck, which I showed to the cast but passed on to Sam as a memento. Olivier was not there himself and we never met him, but I told Sam that Orson Welles was in the audience which amused him greatly. Among our supporters were some Irish actors based in London, my first wife Betty and, slightly the worse for wear, Dominic Behan, the brother of Brendan.

I realised early in the first half that the shipyard slang and Belfast accent were falling on deaf ears. They didn't understand a word of it and none of the shipyard jokes meant a thing; in fact the first act was falling flat on its face when suddenly, Dominic Behan, who was by now gloriously drunk, rose from his seat in the front stalls and yelled: 'It's too good for yis!' It was probably the most riveting moment of the entire evening. I now understood what Guthrie had meant by the 'damp squib' effect. We had none of the build-up of the 'banned play' that had aroused the curiosity of the public in Belfast and Dublin and led to huge audiences. Some of that had filtered through to Glasgow and Edinburgh but none of it featured in our advance publicity for London; and even if it had, the English were just not interested in events in Northern Ireland at that time.

These thoughts were going through my mind when disaster struck. I was observing the action when Scene Two ended and the revolve came into play, a spectacular effect which invariably drew a spontaneous burst of applause from the audience and even the occasional cheer, a response which I encouraged by using the extras as cheerleaders. With sirens blaring and whistles blowing, the scaffolding and huge 'hull' would begin to move and was intended to create the impression of the launching of a ship; but halfway through the movement the whole operation came adrift and the massive superstructure on its now insecure base was sliding in the direction of the orchestra pit. I was out of the box, through the pass door and onto the stage in seconds. I found Henry Lynch Robinson already there in full evening dress and directing operations in full view of the audience. All hands were there pulling on guy ropes or pushing the structure roughly into place for the next scene. A badly shaken Kathleen Feenan who played the part of Marian Mitchell and who had been heard screaming above the mayhem, had been rescued from the top of the staircase and had to be escorted up again. It was pandemonium! Henry vainly attempted to find a place for the next scene that would approximate to the lighting positions but it was a hopeless task because there were no marks, since such a situation had been entirely unforeseen. It transpired that the elderly stagehand positioned under the stage whose job it was to remove the central bolt from its steel socket, had mistimed his cue and pulled the lever too soon.

The entire cast were rather shocked by the incident but managed to hold themselves wonderfully together, especially Kathleen Feenan, marvellous little trooper that she was, who brought her shattered nerves under control and put them to positive good use in a fine performance. Throughout the Belfast and Dublin runs and during our pre-London tour, such a thing had never happened, nor was it seen as likely to happen, not by the remotest chance; and now the impossible had occurred on a West End opening night! It was the very worst of bad luck and lived up to this particular theatre's reputation as a 'graveyard of plays'.

After the show and a desultory ripple of applause from a clearly bored audience, there were a few dressing room drinks, but nearly everyone was anxious to make it to the nearest pub before last orders. There was no formal party and little in the way of first night visitors; Dominic Behan, apparently, had been escorted from the theatre and put in a taxi bound for Balham which is where he lived at the time, but I seem to remember Donal Donnelly, Godfrey Quigley and Norman Rodway coming backstage to congratulate us; or was it to commiserate? Sam, Henry and myself had booked tables for the entire cast at Papa and Mama Olivelli's, a wonderful establishment in Store Street, off the Tottenham Court Road and just a stone's throw away from the theatre. This 'institution', sadly no longer there, was recommended to me by Sam Rayne, an old variety artist known as 'The Irish Playboy'. The arrangement was that if you chose to stay with them you were given a key to your own room, in a building right next door to the restaurant which in any case, was open at all hours. Mama's cooking was traditional Italian and she expected theatre people to be late. Her home cooking was superb 'Mama mia style', and you were never disappointed or made to feel you had outstayed your welcome. I have little memory of that night, but we certainly forgot the disasters of the evening and chose to await the verdict of the following morning's newspapers. Sam and myself who, like several other members of the cast, had keys to rooms, were swept out with the fag ends.

Despite the late night we awoke early, and when I knocked on Sam's door he was washed and shaved and ready to face the morning. We headed for the Tottenham Court Road to find a place to have breakfast, picking up the morning papers at a newsagent's on the way. I cannot now remember in detail any particular reports but they were almost unanimously unfavourable. Strangely enough, one review I do remember, which was one of the better ones, came from Bernard Levin, the critic of the *Daily Express*, but it carried an unfortunate headline which was: 'It takes too long to get *Over The Bridge*'.

Levin was notoriously hard to please but he was kind enough not to mention the scenic disaster. However, the long first part of his review read like an uncompromising 'thumbs down'. 'Were I not a professional critic paid to do my job, I would not have returned to my seat after the interval' it said. 'Had I not done so, however,' it went on, 'I would have missed one of the highlights of the season;' and he went on to elaborate on 'this most moving theatrical experience.' This went some way to cheering Sam up; at least he'd been recognised as a serious writer by a major critic.

Though I was not mentioned as the director of the play, I was singled out for honourable mention in my small cameo role. 'James Ellis as the mob leader,' said Mr Levin, 'shows some of these shamrock flaunting stage Irishmen exactly how it should be done.' I was particularly gratified by this recognition because at that time films, television and the stage were all over-populated by stage Irishmen. It was what the English public wanted to hear and I would have to wait another two years before I could get my foot in the door. Ironically Bernard Levin was to name *Over The Bridge* in a list he called 'My Five Best Plays of the Year', regretting that his review may have contributed to its coming off. We read this rare retraction some months after the event, and, as Sam was to say ruefully, 'It's a bit late for that!'

Meanwhile we had a meeting to attend early that afternoon, which was a Wednesday. Laurier Lister and other representatives of Laurence Olivier Productions were due to attend, as well as Sam, Henry and myself with our respective agents and accountants. The outcome of the meeting was a foregone conclusion and it was just a matter of guessing when the axe would fall. *Johnny the Priest* had lasted for fourteen days; perhaps we might do better but that was a forlorn hope. When the advance bookings were seen to be negligible with little hope of them getting any better, and the running costs of the production were taken into account, the most sensible course of action seemed to be to cut our losses straight away. Consequently it was decided, regrettably but unanimously, to close the play after the Saturday evening performance. After the huge successes of the play in Belfast and Dublin, *Over The Bridge* in the West End was to close after just four performances.

I had intended to end this memoir with the completion of the *Over The Bridge* story but it seemed to me less than honest to leave out the circumstances that accounted for the decline of the company that presented it, ending with the sale to Littlewoods of the Empire Theatre and its eventual demolition early in 1961.

Despite the West End letdown in the wake of the unprecedented triumphs of Belfast and Dublin, we returned home in surprisingly high spirits, having learned some salutary lessons and made some useful contacts in London and elsewhere, including our friends at Laurence Olivier Productions, as well as our prospective producers at Granada, who had bought the television rights to the play and were preparing to screen it nationwide with the legendary Scottish film actor Finlay Currie as Davy Mitchell and the up and coming Donal Donnelly in the role of Peter O'Boyle. On top of this, we had acquired powerful and influential agents in London Management.

Uppermost in my mind, however, were ambitious plans to prepare Sam's second play, *The Evangelist*, for the stage with no stone left unturned to make it even more impressive than his first effort.

Sam Thompson circa 1964.

James Ellis centre, as courtier in Love's Labours Lost *at the Bristol Old Vic.*
Photograph by John Vickers, Courtesy: University of Bristol Theatre Collection.

As O'Grady the Communist with Harold Goldblatt (left) as the priest in Tomeltly's Is The Priest At Home? *(1953)*

James Ellis aged 23 (1954).

Margaret D'Arcy, R.H. McCandless and Catherine Gibson celebrate the Ulster Group Theatre's 18th birthday, 12th March 1958 – © Belfast Telegraph.

Programme for The Country Boy *by John Murphy.*

J. Ritchie McKee.

Henry Lynch Robinson circa 1959.

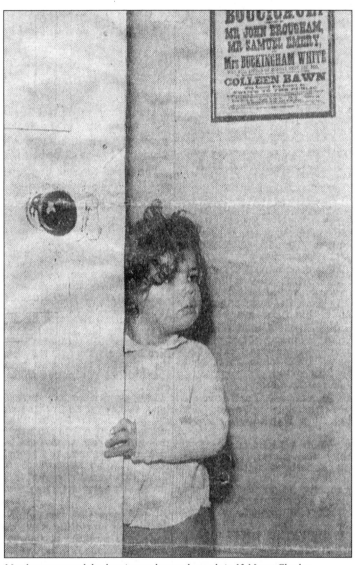

Mandy peeps round the door in wonder at rehearsals in 12 Mount Charles.
© Belfast Telegraph.

OUR NEXT PRESENTATION :

The IRISH PREMIER of

'OVER THE BRIDGE'

A Shipyard Play by SAM THOMPSON

Directed by JAMES ELLIS

FORTHCOMING ATTRACTIONS :

TROUBLE IN THE SQUARE

An Irish Comedy by JACK LOUDAN   Directed by R. H. MacCANDLESS

Original 1959 programme for Over The Bridge.

COMMENCING TUESDAY, 26th JANUARY, 1960

Ulster Bridge Productions Ltd.

presents

J. G. DEVLIN and **JOSEPH TOMELTY**

in the World Premiere of

OVER THE BRIDGE

By SAM THOMPSON

Also starring **Harry Towb**

CAST (in order of appearance)

RABBIE WHITE	J. G. DEVLIN
WARREN BAXTER	HARRY TOWB
Mr. FOX	JAMES BOYCE
GEORGE MITCHELL	CHARLES WITHERSPOON
EPHRAIM SMART	DEREK NICHOLL
ARCHIE KERR	SAM THOMPSON
DAVY MITCHELL	JOSEPH TOMELTY
PETER O'BOYLE	RAY ALCORN
BILLY MORGAN	JOHN McBRIDE
MARIAN MITCHELL	KATHLEEN FEENAN
MARTHA WHITE	IRENE BINGHAM
NELLIE MITCHELL	CATHERINE GIBSON
MOB LEADER	JAMES ELLIS
1st WORKMAN	BILL BENTLEY
2nd WORKMAN	VINCENT KELLY

also featuring

Members of the Lord Carson Memorial Flute Band

THE PLAY PRODUCED BY JAMES ELLIS

Decor and Lighting by Henry Lynch-Robinson

Front Gauze designed by Kenneth Jamison

The Management cannot be responsible for the absence of

Cast list for the 1959 premiere of Over The Bridge.

119

John McBride as Billy Morgan, Sam Thompson as Archie Kerr, Roy Alcorn as Peter Boyle in the first production of Over The Bridge *at the Empire Theatre, 1959.*

Watch It Sailor *poster, 1960.*

James Ellis in Stewart Love's play The Randy Dandy.

Part Two
The Evangelist and its Aftermath

The Evangelist – A Synopsis
by James Ellis

Finlay Bradford, a corrupt but 'born again' contractor, has built a new
gospel hall – with men and materials stolen from other jobs – and has
invited Pastor Earls, an American evangelist and faith healer, to appear
for a celebration week to mark the occasion. The preacher will be an
honoured guest in the builder's house which is virtually next door. On
the other side of the composite setting is the snug of Connery's public
house, leaving the entire forestage to serve as the street itself. It is in
these acting areas that the opening scenes of the play take place,
introducing two of the key characters who will have major parts in the
action and its rather predictable dénouement.

Manser Brown, as well as being a confirmed agnostic, is a brother
of Finlay Bradford's wife and therefore an uncle to their two children.
Still a bachelor, Brown lives in the Bradford house and works for
Bradford's firm. When we meet Manser, he is drinking with his cronies
until one of them upsets him by casting aspersions on his nephew,
Johnny, who is in poor health and has spent most of his young life in
hospitals. Manser, who is extremely fond of the lad, storms out of the
pub. On the street, he bumps into Johnny who has temporarily
absconded from the hospital. Failing to persuade him to return, they

have a drink together before he makes one last attempt to call him a taxi, as Johnny walks off into the darkness of the wings.

At the climax of the gospel hall scene, however, after the rousing hymns, the testimonies, the persuasive oratory of the evangelist and right in the midst of the hypnotic healing process itself, Johnny, in tears, approaches the platform to embrace his father and mother and plead for help. It takes little effort from Pastor Earls to persuade the boy to accept the Lord Jesus Christ as his personal Saviour and to submit his ailing body to the healer's apparently God-given powers. Seemingly 'cured', the miracle boy, along with his healer, is borne shoulder high from the gospel hall to the strains of 'Marching to Zion'.

Manser is staggering back from the pub when he hears the congregation approach. He enters the house and locks the door. After a long scene in which Manser defies Pastor Earls and a hysterical crowd, he emerges to face the preacher's challenge to cast out his devils. In the rather undignified sequence that follows, three of Earls' followers grab hold of Manser while the evangelist intones his incantations over the helpless agnostic. The scene ends with the crowd singing hysterically as the lights slowly fade and the curtain falls for the end of Act One.

Act Two consists of four scenes which take place alternately in Finlay Bradford's house and in the street outside. The first scene, which takes place two days after the spectacular and amazingly theatrical meeting in the gospel hall, opens with a reporter interviewing the evangelist while a photographer takes pictures of the miracle boy and his healer for a local newspaper. That over, Earls begins planning for a large scale healing rally to be held at the magnificent King's Hall where Johnny will testify to his miraculous conversion and cure.

The protagonists in the play are divided into two camps; on the one hand, the 'born again' believers led by Earls and his cronies, and on the other, the sceptics, led by Manser Brown, who undoubtedly represents the views of the author himself. This tedious wrangle goes on for far too long and is only relieved by moments of tenderness between a plainly confused Johnny and his obviously caring nurse, Norah, who has turned up to persuade him to return to the hospital. These scenes, and another touching cameo where at Johnny's request Manser sings the hymn, 'O love that will not let me go', are welcome distractions in the rather predictable march to a predictable tragic ending. Before it actually happens, however, some ugly scenes occur in which Manser's somewhat aggressive agnosticism seems to assert itself as absolute truth. Harsh words are exchanged between Finlay Bradford and Manser who has told Johnny that his parents had tried to have him adopted when he was born. This revelation may make Manser feel better though it is unlikely to have a similar effect on Johnny. The end is signalled by Norah screaming, 'Oh! Johnny, my poor Johnny', and by her coming to the door, sobbing bitterly. Johnny's death is confirmed by Manser appearing at the upstairs window and slowly drawing the blind.

I

Based on the religious revival in Ulster of 1859, *The Evangelist* focuses on the exploitation of working class people by a corupt evangelical creature. We discussed even at that stage the possibility of engaging a star performer, an actor whose charisma would capture the platform presence of Sam's leading character, Pastor John Earls, and effortlessly transmit his magic as an evangelical preacher and faith healer. The names Sam Wanamaker and even Laurence Olivier himself were discussed but when I re-read the still rough draft of the play, I made it quite clear to Sam that there would be no question of forwarding it for consideration at this stage. Actors of such stature would turn the part down out of hand, I said, and there might be no second chance of persuading them to change their minds.

My first positive response was that the preacher should have a backup platform party of singers and instrumentalists to underscore his mesmeric presence and its hypnotic effect on his congregation. Sam had no first-hand experience of the Gospel Hall scene and likewise little time for 'bible thumpers' of any creed and colour. In fact his response to what he regarded as credulous believers might be summed up in his often repeated remark: 'There's nothin' over the wall.'

I, on the other hand, had experienced the world of religious rallies, tent meetings and gospel halls as a child and teenager, when my mother had dragged myself and my father round these venues in her unremitting search for truth. What remained with me, and still has, was the almost hypnotic effect of the hymns and gospel songs, such as 'Only Believe', 'There is Power in the Blood' and 'We're Marching to Zion'. These, I thought, and any more I could call to mind, would give the production something of the quality of a musical, or even a musical drama and would involve the audience in a certain degree of participation that could well be infectious. With that thought in mind, I looked through revival hymnbooks in my parents' house before I took

Sam on a tour of likely gospel halls in East Belfast where we listened, outside the premises at first, to the clearly audible sounds of worship and rousing hymns, punctuated by loud cries of 'Amen', 'Hallelujah' and 'Praise the Lord'. Sam had the idea of going to hear Dr Ian Paisley speak at the Ulster Hall and, though I had reservations about this, we went just the same. I felt that Paisley's Ulster 'persona' was already too close to Sam's portrayal of the transatlantic preacher who at this stage seemed to know his way around Belfast like a native and could refer to local football teams with a familiarity that was totally out of character. Our visit to the Reverend Paisley's rally confirmed my worst fears. The proceedings had more of a sectarian undercurrent with a largely anti-papacy theme, and although 'Big Ian's' aggressive oratory was in its way impressive, I pointed out to Sam, quite forcibly, that it was not what we were looking for. You must, I insisted, seek diligently for an unmistakably American persona for your evangelist.

Some time later, alerted by eye-catching advertisements in the summer of 1960, we paid another visit to the Ulster Hall which I hoped would inspire Sam to redouble his efforts. The advertisement was as follows:

"Assemblies of God Pentecostal Church
(Underneath this heading is a photograph)
HEAR THIS MAN OF FAITH AND POWER.
HEAR HIS SOUL-SAVING, BODY-HEALING,
REVIVAL MINISTRY.
COMING TO BELFAST
Evangelists PAUL and BETTY WELLS
from USA
Bring the halt, lame, blind and the so-called incurables."

We were not disappointed by the astonishing spectacle as we listened attentively to the music and witnessed the spell-binding performance of Paul Wells in particular. This was exactly what I wanted Sam, and of course myself, to experience.

Now, I hoped, we could press ahead and finish the job. Sam had been a guest of Lord Killanin who had lent him a house on his estate at Spiddal in County Galway. Sam returned from this 'working holiday' with some 'improvements', but thought he was too far removed from his usual environment to be either relaxed or totally concentrated; and, to be honest, I was not entirely happy with the progress he had made. May Thompson seems to remember that Sam returned home from the Ulster hall with a record made by the evangelical duo which cost seven pounds ten shillings, an enormous sum for those days, but I don't recall that particular detail.

One worry, or rather reservation, was that I felt Sam identified too closely with the character of the agnostic Manser Brown, a role he was to take himself when the play was eventually staged at the Opera House in June, 1963. His own personal catchphrase – 'There's nothin' over the wall' – became a frequently recurring leitmotif in Manser's vocabulary and at the time I certainly had no quarrel with that; but back in 1960 there was never any suggestion of the author himself playing the part. I would almost certainly have thought that Sam was too inexperienced for such an undertaking and he himself might well have been overawed at the thought of playing 'the Devil's advocate' opposite a major star; at least I like to think so. What concerned me more was that the dice were loaded in favour of Manser and against the evangelist even before the latter had failed to 'deliver the goods', thereby, certainly at that stage, turning Sam's second play into a satire or even a melodrama as against the more impartial handling of *Over The Bridge*, where the playwright expressed himself as an insider and eyewitness rather than as a completely uninformed sceptic. Manser Brown, for example, could have been more accurately described as an atheist rather than an agnostic; but I suppose I could be accused of splitting hairs.

In an effort to steer Sam away from too simplistic an approach, I drew his attention at this time to an article by the Reverend Doctor W.R.

Matthews, the Dean of St Pauls, which appropriately appeared on a Saturday and on the very same page of the *Belfast Telegraph* as the multiplicity of advertisements for the following day's attractions at the many and varied gospel halls in the city. The article was headed 'Why so many religions?' and I quote from it:

> "There are so many versions of the Christian faith and so many flocks which profess to belong to Christ. The question 'which one?' inevitably arises and blunts the sharpness of the appeal to the spirit of the inquirer.
>
> "Could it be that in the Providence of God these two problems of multiplicity are meant to stir up our minds and lead us to the perception that they are closely related ..."

He goes on to argue that there will be little success with the conversion of the world until we (The Church, I presume) have "attained unity ourselves".

Sam's response was to say, with some vehemence, that there was little chance of that happening in Belfast and I have to admit that I agreed with him; not before insisting, however, that he had to be a little more even-handed in the portrayal of his leading character and pointing out that the second half of the play was a bit weak, over-written and something of an anti-climax. All this, I must say, was taken on the chin by Sam as we set to work together in the front parlour of his house in Craigmore Street. I remember remarking to Sam at the time that we could learn something from these unwavering believers as far as publicity and self-advertisement were concerned and thought we should let it be known when the time was right and the script was ready, that *The Evangelist* would be a better play and even more sensational than *Over The Bridge*. By this time we had become very close friends as well as colleagues and I do not think that I ever experienced a more congenial working relationship.

131

II

One part of my brief as a director of Findlater & Company was to collaborate with the theatre manager, Frank Reynolds, in changing the image of the old Empire from that of a music hall or variety venue to a place where the public could expect to see plays of a decent, and certainly professional standard while Ulster Bridge Productions was re-grouping after the ambitious and, as it transpired, variable touring expeditions to Dublin, Scotland and England.

The couple of months we had spent away were a transition period for our new home during which the theatre tried to raise the standard of its visiting variety artistes in competition with the old Group. In a desperate attempt to save face the old Group had invited the comedian James Young to replace the ineffectual Jonathan Goodman and run what was euphemistically called a 'Theatre of Comedy' employing non Equity supporting artists, (he, himself had been banned from the actors trade union). To cap it all, and to the particular fury of J.G. Devlin who was the union's area representative, Young's 'company' was quite improperly supported by funds from CEMA, money which he boasted about paying back in full at the end of his tenure, for which gesture he was publicly applauded by his self-satisfied chairman, J. Ritchie McKee. Now I know that in his day James Young was undoubtedly a comic genius and he has left behind some recorded sketches that will ensure his enduring fame and that have become over the years collectors' items portraying Belfast characters both male and female, to be enjoyed by generations who never saw him in the flesh. Nevertheless, his sojourn at the Group Theatre with what was so obviously an opportunistic move at the expense of fellow thespians was not I believe his finest hour and earned him nothing but their contempt at his stance in what has turned out to be one of the most crucial struggles for survival in Northern Ireland's, if not the whole of Ireland's, theatre history.

On our return to Belfast, Frank, the theatre's amiable manager, filled me in on what had transpired during our absence. I do not remember much of what he told me but I seem to have a not very reliable note somewhere that in early May, an ever popular revival of *Old Time Music Hall* starring G.H. Elliott, Randolph Sutton and others, took place. I know my father would have made an effort to see these 'old-timers' for he often mentioned other famous names, such as Burlington Bertie, Vesta Tilley, Gertie Gitana and many more. Edwin Heath, the famous hypnotist also appeared at the Empire around the same time and I remember hinting to Sam that he was perhaps not unlike an evangelist in his ability to effortlessly mesmerise large groups of people.

On the 14 June, 1960, a company from Dublin, directed by Godfrey Quigley and starring Cyril Cusack in a double bill of Shaw's *Arms and the Man* with Samuel Beckett's *Krapps Last Tape* was due to open but the elaborate settings by the world famous and much in demand Sean Kenny could not be erected without the designer's presence and he had been delayed by last minute business to do with another engagement at a London theatre I believe. Cyril refused to appear before black drapes and so the first night had to be cancelled. The actor explained that he would not insult his audience by accepting such a compromise, and an announcement was made offering ticket holders their money back or seats for another night. Thinking on my feet, I rang Ulster Television and explained the situation. Cyril was by then an established star of stage and screen who had particularly endeared himself to the Belfast public with a wonderful performance in the film *Odd Man Out* and especially by his flawless delivery of an authentic Belfast accent, so the producers had no hesitation in snapping up the possibility of his appearance on UTV. I was asked to appear with him and immediately approached the actor. I asked him if he would repeat the reason for his non-appearance and he readily agreed. In the ensuing live interview he stated quite unequivocally, and with the customary Cusack charm, that his non-appearance that night was entirely down to the fact that he would not insult a knowledgeable Belfast audience by performing on a bare stage. He explained that the designer, who was crucial to the production, was on his way and Cyril would appear the following night. Then he added with a disarming smile: 'And of course for the entire week.' Needless to say, he played to packed houses. The critic Betty Lowry described his dual performance in her review as: "More than a demonstration of his versatility. It is a tour de force!"

The following week saw the arrival of Michael MacLiammoir who appeared in an American melodrama written in 1844 and called *The Drunkard*, but by then Frank Reynolds and myself had been dispatched across the channel by the Findlaters to find a suitable repertory company, partly to fill the awkward summer months and partly to give Ulster Bridge Productions breathing space. They were also aware that Sam was struggling to complete his next play and were particularly concerned about my difficult position as a director of their Dublin company and my obligations to Ulster Bridge Productions. I believe I had prompted the idea at one of their board meetings by mentioning that my former boss at the Group Theatre, Harold Goldblatt had addressed a similar problem by arranging a summer season at Colchester while their repertory company had appeared in Belfast. Whatever the reason, Dermot Findlater at once seized on the idea and took immediate action.

And so it transpired that Frank and yours truly found ourselves in north Wales taking note of what was on offer at the holiday resorts. The only company I can clearly recall was the Galleon Theatre at Llandudno but to be honest we thought it was no better than the best of a bad bunch; and besides, none of them seemed to have had the resources to provide a second company. We decided to report back and seek permission to move on. I remembered I had heard or read favourable accounts, (possibly in the actor's newspaper, *The Stage*), of a company or companies based on the south coast of England; and at one and the

134

same time the resort of Bexhill-on-Sea together with the names Richard Burnett and Peggy Paige sprung to mind. After Frank had phoned Dublin, we caught a train to London with instructions to stay at the Piccadilly Hotel, which had been thoughtfully arranged by the firm, and the following morning an amusing incident occurred.

A telegram money order which was addressed to me arrived at the reception desk and I set off to cash it in Regent Street. The amount on the order was one hundred pounds and the cashier did not ask me for identification but merely required to know the name and address of the sender. I tried Mr Findlater but when that didn't work, I offered the name of the managing director Mr John McGrail which got me no further. 'By the way,' said the friendly cashier 'you haven't quite got the address right either. Would you like to have another go?' 'Surely it's O'Connell Street', I said. 'I know it like the back of my hand – it's known as Findlater's Corner.' 'Ah, maybe that explains it,' said the helpful man behind the counter. 'Don't tell me it's in the street running off O'Connell Street,' I said, getting more and more desperate. 'If so, I haven't got a clue!' 'It's not that difficult', said my helpful friend, 'you're just missing one word.' At last, the penny dropped as I exclaimed, to the amusement of some of the queue behind me, 'Upper O'Connell Street!' Now there was just the small matter of the name of the sender. 'It's a lady's name,' said my friend. It must be Mary, the firm's secretary, I thought, but I hadn't a clue what her surname was except that I presumed it was Irish. I tried every name I could think of in roughly alphabetical order – O'Brien, O'Connell, Daly, O'Farrell, and so on, until I got to O'Reilly ... 'You're nearly there', said the man behind the counter. 'Reilly?' I enquired in desperation. 'It says here, Miss M. Reilly', he said with a broad smile and handed over the money.

We got to Bexhill via Eastbourne early in the afternoon and managed quite quickly to track down Mr Burnett and his charming actress wife, Peggy Paige. We arranged to see them perform that evening in what I seem to remember was an Agatha Christie play and the standard of the entire company was rather good. We went backstage to congratulate them, joined them for a drink and made an appointment for the following afternoon. Before bidding them good-night and arranging accommodation with their assistance, we had made them aware of the purpose of our visit and Mr Burnett, who we now knew as 'Dickie', said he was sure something could be arranged after he had made a few phone calls. The following day a definite commitment was made, though neither he nor his wife could be a part of the deal due to their regular season at the South Coast resort. However, a man called Michael Cooper, who Burnett worked with regularly and could thoroughly recommend, would be free to form an ensemble which would be an offshoot of the parent company 'Penguin Players'. I left the financial arrangements to Frank and the deal was virtually finalised between Richard Burnett's production company and the Findlater organisation. Our mission was accomplished and we caught a mid-evening train, changing at Eastbourne to the *Brighton Belle*, then still a glamorous relic of Edwardian England with private compartments and waiter service where we had a few drinks to celebrate and a late evening supper consisting of a mushroom omelette, bacon, chipolata sausage and black pudding.

I dimly recall only a couple of plays from their repertoire, which were, if my memory serves me right, *Not in the Book* which, starring Wilfred Hyde White, had run for two years in London's West End, and *The Hollow* by Agatha Christie whose plays were very favoured by repertory companies at that time before her complete revival in recent years. In the summer of 1960, however, almost all my attention was focussed on Sam, and preparing, in the face of my underlying fears, to open our own season with an alternative programme, if *The Evangelist* was not ready in time.

III

It was my view then, and still is, that at that time Sam's play was unwieldy and structurally unsound. It was also, in spite of our diligent research and my attempts to instil a degree of empathy for the complex world of Pentecostal fervour, probably well beyond the playwright's field of comprehension and experience. This, undoubtedly, accounted for Sam's total alignment with the sceptics under the leadership of Manser Brown. This particular flaw was creating an imbalance at the very core of the drama, making the eventual outcome all too predictable, especially bearing in mind that the vast majority of a theatre going public, even in Belfast, was unlikely to have had much close contact with the Gospel Hall scene. It was, I felt, our prime duty to seduce and entertain them, allowing the star performer to lull them into a 'willing suspension of disbelief' and allow his charisma and powers of leadership to pervade the Bradford household, but above all, disguise his underlying charlatanism to the very last minute; even then, perhaps, allow his leading character to leave the stage with some dignity and obvious remorse.

In the Bank Bar (now gone) in Bankmore Street, we would swop stories where, because of the theme of the new play, Sam would often ask me about some of my personal experiences. One thing he was particularly curious about was that I had spent a year, (one which included my twenty first birthday), in a sanatorium suffering from a mild form of tuberculosis, from which, due to new drugs and complete bed rest, I happily recovered. Now we had already decided that Johnny, the sickly son of the Bradfords who was to be miraculously 'cured' by the evangelist, should be a chronic consumptive, well advanced in the illness before his apparent healing, but Sam was interested to hear any 'inside stories' that might embellish his play. I don't know at what stage we shared the following yarns but I suspect it was quite early in our talks.

I was highly amused on re-reading the play after an interval of some fifty years to find a few references to these stories in the very first scene. Here is example one:

> JOBBER: Do you know that git Bradford has told people that the Lord is punishing his son for his sins …

Well I told Sam that an elder of my dear mother's church told me exactly the same thing – needless to say, my mother was furious – Here is another:

> JOHNNY: I got a treble up on the horses today, Manser. It run me to twenty quid. I got you a present. (he produces a bottle of whisky from his pocket.)
>
> MANSER: How the hell could you get a treble up when you're in hospital?
>
> JOHNNY: A fellow in the next ward runs a book; everybody's in on it …
>
> (winks), even the male staff.

Well, we were so bored in the hospital; one frustration was that although we could read the racing pages in the newspapers, we couldn't have a flutter. For that matter, neither could we afford it. Anyway, by way of recreation, a fellow called Jim McGann and myself, must have accumulated a very limited amount of cash between us and decided to open a 'Penny Book' with a kitty that amounted to only ten shillings and accept bets of no more than a penny. Unfortunately somebody persuaded us on the very first day to accept a penny 'Yankee' which is six doubles, four trebles and an accumulator and every single horse came up, thereby taking more than our entire kitty. Stuck for funds and unable to pay in full, an older man in the ward bailed us out on condition he became a one third shareholder. Strangely enough I met him on a cross channel ferry some considerable time afterwards and he told me he had been in the hospital for another four years after we left and had saved enough to take his wife on a world cruise. These stories are an entire diversion but they illustrate, I think, the close bond between Sam and myself and how he could incorporate material from life into his own work.

The third example of this aspect of subliminal 'collaboration' was, I believe, instrumental in arousing Sam's creative impulses and developing one of the happiest and most moving themes in his plot, the romantic attachment of Johnny and Norah, the 'wee night nurse':

MANSER: I don't want to see you getting into trouble, Johnny. Will they not miss you at the hospital?
JOHNNY: (forcing a smile.) That's been taken care of, Manser. It's recreation night. All the patients are up at a film show in the main hall. Anyway, I'm well in with the wee night nurse ...

I had told Sam of another daring escapade, aimed at countering the boredom and loss of freedom we felt at being confined, it seemed indefinitely, in hospital. Another patient called John Lightbody and myself had chatted up a couple of pretty nurses and persuaded them to come with us to a dance hall. This, of course, involved us escaping through a window after 'lights out' when the night sister had come on duty and apparently done her rounds; but in case she came back we had arranged bolsters and pillows to simulate sleeping figures. We returned undetected after midnight and somebody opened a window to let us in. After a last minute snog we climbed back into the ward and promptly fell asleep. The romantic attachments did not survive our discharge from hospital but I still remember the name of my wee nurse.

None of this, however, compensated for what I still considered were the major flaws in Sam's second effort for the stage. The hoped for production which was to be the mainstay of our autumn season was in my view fast becoming an unrealistic dream. I had already made not entirely satisfactory contingency plans in the event of the play not being

139

ready but I decided to make one last effort by persuading Sam to allow me to collaborate with him. The plan was that he should concentrate on making the second half of the play less clumsy and predictable, attempting where possible to cut any irrelevant or over wordy passages and ensuring that his evangelist at least 'appeared' to maintain his unshakeable self-belief almost to the final curtain; the idea of having the dénouement at the King's Hall rally we dismissed as unrealistic and impractical.

I undertook the task of 'Americanising' pastor Earls and re-organising the Gospel Hall scene, carefully choosing the hymns and omitting, where I felt it unnecessary, invitations for the audience to join in; the platform party of singers and instrumentalists should instinctively know their cues and the entire operation should be slick and thoroughly professional. Furthermore, I felt that the local pastors should be given a little less opportunity to upstage the star performer, no matter how droll these comic caricatures seemed to their creator.

We set to work agreeably on the floor of the house in Craigmore Street with me assuring Sam that I was doing no more than what I thought was my job and there was no question of my claiming part authorship of the play. It was just an extension of our modus operandi for *Over The Bridge* with the added burden of working against the clock, plus the far more ambitious and complex scenario. The added difficulty, as I have said, was that Sam was working for the first time outside the sphere of his immediate experience.

A main concern was to place the gospel hymns in their most effective sequence but I chose to arrange this after I had agreed the build-up to the entrance of the American pastor which I assured Sam was an excellent sequence, culminating in the catchphrase 'Bible days are here again' and the hymns 'Bringing in the Sheaves' and 'The Lord's move is on'. This, together with the opening scene which introduced two key characters in Manser Brown and Johnny, had created most effectively an air of expectancy and conflict – a promising start which did not, alas, as things stood, finally deliver the goods. I thought the gospel hall scene could be made with a little effort on my part, a really exciting piece of theatre, more spectacular even than *Over The Bridge*, and I was eagerly looking forward to directing it; but it would fall flat on its face unless Sam completely re-worked the second half of his play. I began my contribution by concentrating on the preacher's particular brand of transatlantic oratory and stressing the commercial imagery of his sermon from the outset. I have kept a copy of the play that dates from this time (1960) and it differs hardly at all from the published version which is presumably more or less identical to the play as performed at the Grand Opera House, Belfast, on 3rd June 1963. Along with the interesting cast list, which included that fine actor, Ray McAnally, and Sam himself, it records that the play was 'devised and directed' by Hilton Edwards, whatever that meant! It can only mean that when Sam eventually found a director in Hilton, he presented him with the very same version that we had worked on three years earlier and which had never found its way onto the stage of the Empire Theatre. Any claim to have 'devised' the play can only refer to the staging or mise-en-scène, and nothing more.

But to return to the script of 1960 and the elaborate plans to stage it. Eventually, I began as I say with the preacher's oration, starting with the words, "This is the competitive age", and continuing ...

"It's the age of super salesmanship and high pressure publicity. It glares at you from every neon sign and every newspaper. It glares at you from every cinema screen and television set ... Satan has bought and owns all the best sites. His bright lights glitter outside his movie theatres, his dance halls and bingo halls and so on ...

"Today, people are brainwashed by every detergent on the market. Washing powders that add brightness to whiteness or it's the whiteness that catches the eye! Let me tell you friends,

there's nothing so sparkling or so white as a soul that's been washed in the Blood of the Lamb! He leaves no stains ...
(everyone shouts 'Hallelujah!' and the choir needs no prompting to sing)
"There is power, power, wonder-working power, in the blood of the Lamb ..."

This is a prime example of what I meant by pastor Earls not having to interrupt his flow by stopping to invite his congregation to join in, (e.g. 'Let's sing a verse of it', 'Let us raise the roof, etc.') Such unnecessary interpolations still remain in the published text, as well as the largely unaltered and unsatisfactory second half of the play. I have always maintained that *The Evangelist* was to a very great extent unfinished business, a verdict I passed on to Maura Megahy without mentioning at the time my own personal input; and though I regret not seeing the play, if only to have seen Ray McAnally in the leading role, I have had no reason to change that opinion.

At the time, however, I tended to push such doubts to the back of my mind and press on with future planning. I checked out the business commitments of Henry Lynch Robinson who was a busy architect much in demand and found that he already had more than enough on his plate including plans to mount an elaborate Christmas pantomime for which he was not only designing the set, but was fully engaged in writing the book. We discussed the situation and I think it may have been he who mentioned the name of my cousin, Kenneth Jamison, who had designed and painted a front-gauze for the setting of *Over The Bridge* and had, moreover, designed a number of notable settings for the Arts Theatre. Certain that I was not stepping on Henry's toes, I now approached Kenneth with two propositions, one was to design a setting for Joseph Tomelty's play, *A Shilling for the Evil Day*, which was to be a much improved version of *All Soul's Night* with a more credible ending and secondly, to design and make a model for *The Evangelist*.

The first project was easily explained and could for the moment be postponed. The model for Sam's play was a much more demanding challenge and Kenneth picked up the gauntlet straight away and began producing highly creative sketches in his bold, inimitable style. Hour after hour was spent often late into the night. It was challenging work but intensely rewarding and was largely instrumental in forming my overall approach to the planned production. One comic episode which Kenneth and myself often recall with some amusement is that in helping to construct the model, I managed to slice a part of my middle finger off with a Stanley knife. These, and many other memories, we share on my visits back to Belfast but the finer details of that setting are hard to recall and the model, despite numerous attempts to recreate its basic structure, alas, no longer exists.

Work on *The Evangelist* continued. I concentrated on the musical side of the production, in particular proposing to Sam certain hymns for key moments, aiming more for maximum emotional response, and of course histrionic effect, rather than any hint of ridicule. I pointed to the wisdom and inspiration of his personal choice of the hymn 'O Love That Will Not Let Me Go' to be sung by Manser, the agnostic, to his newly converted nephew, Johnny, and suggested there were also examples of genuine emotion and real fervour to be underscored in the scene in the Gospel Hall. I recommended that 'There is Power in the Blood' should be allowed to speak for itself, without inciting the audience to 'join in', but during the healing process, economy was the secret. The evangelist's very presence was charismatic. I remembered a particularly beautiful hymn to underscore the scene as the sick gathered round:

> At even when the sun was set, the sick, O Lord, around Thee lay,
> Oh, in what divers pains they met! Oh, with what joy they
> went away!
> (This to be sung by the backing group as the healing line
> assembled)

From the published version of *The Evangelist*, it seems that pastor Earls himself led the singing of this hymn at the end of the healing session, so I assume that was the choice in Hilton Edward's production. Sam and myself, after a lot of work and occasional disagreements, had on the whole come to mutually acceptable terms. I remember only one dangerous moment, when the two of us were agonising over this particular scene and I was scribbling furiously in an attempt to present the American as a super salesman for God. Sam looked up from his own work on the second half of the play to ask, 'Who's writing this play? Me or you?' I looked him straight in the eye and replied, 'We are, Sam,' and the subject was never raised again.

IV

As the days and weeks went by, it became clear that Sam's play would not be fit for production until the New Year at the earliest. Even then there was the added headache of finding a star, if he was free, and persuading him to come to Belfast, even if we could convince Laurence Olivier Productions that the play was ready for the stage and we could count on their support; an important consideration in mounting what was obviously going to be a very expensive undertaking. Reluctantly, I shared my misgivings with Sam and Henry who, after due consideration supported my plans for an alternative programme for the months of October and November, though Sam was understandably disappointed. This of course meant that Henry and myself would be fully occupied for at least three months, leaving Sam completely free to concentrate on his second major play. I thought at the time that this was probably for the best and after one last effort to motivate him, I, by and large, left him to get on with it, emphasising once more that he was to concentrate all his attention on the second half of his script.

It is common knowledge that by postponing the production of the play, I did not stay to witness the demolition of the old Empire Theatre and was obviously not free to direct it; which of course was a bitter disappointment. After all the work that Sam, myself and Kenneth Jamison had put into its preparation, I never did see the play in the theatre but was naturally keen to follow Sam's efforts to have it staged. Amongst all the postponements and to-ings and fro-ings, which must have been a constant strain for Sam, there is one encounter where I would have dearly loved to have been a fly on the wall and that was when Sam met Hilton Edwards to discuss his play. John Keyes mentions that Hilton 'was anxious that Thompson might find his bluff English accent and manner patronising.' I have often wondered whether either man referred to the stormy encounter involving Orson Welles in Alfredo's night club.

Meanwhile, back in the autumn of 1960, there was a programme of plays to be decided upon and a company of players to be engaged, some on a freelance basis and others on longer term contracts. J.G. Devlin, for example opted to make himself available for certain plays when the dates did not clash with his London commitments, especially for television for which he was then much in demand. By contrast, I have still in my possession a press cutting from the *Belfast Telegraph* dated Tuesday, 17th September, showing Elizabeth Begley and Kathleen Feenan with myself in attendance, signing six month contracts over lunch in the Grand Central Hotel in Royal Avenue. Other members of the old Group Theatre who would have signed similar contracts at the same time must have included Margaret D'Arcy, Catherine Gibson and Doreen Hepburn, as well as Maurice O'Callaghan, John McBride and possibly Sean Reid.

The first play of the new season was Joseph Tomelty's *All Soul's Night*, re-titled because of considerable changes to the structure and staging, *A Shilling for the Evil Day*. It was favourably reviewed by the critic Tom Carson who described it as "a worthy opening" and particularly noted the changes to the third act which he had previously considered the weakest part of the play. He also commented on the lighting, which along with some appropriate music I had used to make the appearance of the ghosts more atmospheric and believable. Kenneth Jamison's evocative setting had a gauzed back wall which became transparent to evoke a picture of the sea bed with the shell of a fishing boat that rocked to and fro in the current; and it was there that the no longer living wraiths of the brothers Michael and Stephen encountered one another, as their mother, played by Elizabeth Begley started awake with a piercing scream which startled the audience into a willing suspension of disbelief – a scene which in previous productions had produced nothing but embarrassed laughter. In a noteworthy example of such an effort, one of the ghostly brothers had been portrayed by James Young holding a green torch under his chin, so perhaps the laughter was understandable. Outstanding performances on this occasion which were praised by Carson included J.G. Devlin, Elizabeth Begley and Kathleen Feenan.

I think I was as proud of this production of Joe Tomelty's finest play as of anything I have done. It was greatly enhanced by Kenneth Jamison's deceptively simple set and tremendous work from my stage director, Peter Badger, who scoured the Ards Peninsula for suitable props and stage dressing and made friends with the fishing community which had been the inspiration for the story. He returned from his day trip with a lorry load of lobster pots and many other furnishings and artefacts and of course suggested we repay their generosity by organising a bus and complementary tickets for the opening night. This was done, followed by an unforgettable party to mark the occasion, for, needless to say, Joseph Tomelty was a very special local hero among his own people.

Watch it Sailor, billed as the hilarious sequel to *Sailor Beware*, may have seemed a strange choice to follow Tomelty's masterpiece but what with our losses in London and still no sign of *The Evangelist* being remotely ready for production, we had to keep a weather eye on the advance bookings and woo a proverbially fickle theatre-going public with a carefully chosen programme of popular plays. *Sailor Beware* had been a phenomenal success in its adaptation to the Ulster idiom, running for a full six months at the Group Theatre with Elizabeth Begley outstanding in the lead role. Indeed one of its authors, Philip King, was so curious to find out where his unexpected royalties were coming from that he flew to Belfast late in the run to see his play. Utterly perplexed but fully aware that the audience were loving it, he came backstage to congratulate the cast, and especially Elizabeth, expressing his delight and dismay with the unforgettable words 'Marvellous! Absolutely marvellous! Who wrote it?'

With this vivid memory at the forefront of my mind I decided to exploit Elizabeth's considerable and varied range of talents to the full by contrasting her grim and tragic figure in the Tomelty play with her inimitable flair for comedy. At this time I had acquired the services of the talented Desmond Kinney, a fine local artist graphic designer who was a friend of mine and whose job it was to publicise our plays and, as it happens, I still have in my possession the playbill which actually promoted this particular production. Apart from the visual impact which in itself is impressive, (including a wonderful caricature of the actress and cartoons of other cast members), it provides some useful, one might almost say archival information concerning dates and admission prices – research material which is often overlooked:

EMPIRE THEATRE
COMMENCING MONDAY OCT 17th
NIGHTLY at 8 p.m. SAT. at 6.15 & 8.45.
Reserved, six shillings, four and sixpence, three and sixpence,
Gallery two shillings
ELIZABETH BEGLEY IN HER FUNNIEST ROLE

These admission prices were obviously the same as for *Over The*

Bridge which I believe I already knew, but it's reassuring to have it confirmed.

It was now time to concentrate on the pantomime, *Cinderella*, for which we had made a futile attempt to book Belfast's sweetheart, Ruby Murray who was then top of the hit parade with the song 'Softly Softly' and had at the same time a half dozen other numbers in the charts. During the summer Henry and myself had travelled to Blackpool in a vain effort to persuade Ruby to return to her native city but, alas, it was too late; she had already been contracted by the Grade brothers to appear at Torquay. Now we were under some pressure to find someone else.

At around this time I had made the acquaintance of an old variety artist by the name of Sam Rayne who originally came from Belfast but had spent his entire working life in England. He had been a comedian who appeared under the name 'The Irish Playboy' though ironically he seemed to have adopted a North of England accent in which he would jokingly claim to have learned his trade and done his apprenticeship at Buxton Repertory Company. Sadly, back home in Belfast, no-one would believe the old boy's stories; but I sensed a ring of truth about his past and came to learn a little about his background. He dropped quite a few famous names in his conversation and claimed, as well as topping the bill at some well-known venues, to have been the first comedian to have stepped across the footlights in order to take the audience into his confidence. After a few drinks he would sometimes demonstrate this technique and I must say it was quite believable and convincing. He said his real name was Sam Cochrane and that he was living with his sister on the Antrim Road I believe. I asked him if he had any connections across the water and he replied that all 'Show Business' was centred in London and he could probably look up one or two old acquaintances. I decided to 'call his bluff', if that is not an unkind way of putting it.

I told him about the pantomime and that we were having some

trouble finding suitable stars to top the bill. I also hinted that he himself might consider playing the part of the baron and even assisting with the production itself. More urgently, I wondered if he would at all contemplate a trip to London to sound out some Variety agents who might possibly solve our problems. His face lit up at the thought and a few days later we set off. Heading for the Piccadilly Hotel we found there was a queue for reservations. Unfazed, Sam said 'Leave this to me.' So saying, he placed a rolled up ten shilling note in the palm of his hand and summoned the head porter with a gesture which discreetly exposed the note to view, and immediately attracted undivided attention. 'My friend and I require two single rooms for several days and will be in the Eros Bar for the next half hour', he said, as he thrust the ten shilling note discreetly into the porter's hand. Needless to say he appeared in a matter of minutes with his mission accomplished. I had of course arranged for Sam to have a float to cover immediate expenses and we set off to explore the West End. Sam, I remember, was wearing a rather threadbare overcoat with an Astrakhan collar and a faded but rather well cut navy blue suit, all of which gave the impression of a once celebrated old trouper. Over the next few days I was to witness this old variety artist back in his element; though whether he could produce the goods was something I had to be patient about.

Our first port of call was Jack Solomons' club, though what the famous boxing promoter had to do with our business in London I had no idea. Confronted by doormen who wanted to know if we were members, Sam removed his overcoat and thrust it into the face of one of them, enquiring imperiously if Jack was in, whilst at the same time displaying the apparently obligatory ten bob note. Ushered into the restaurant we were shown to a prominent table and had an excellent lunch. Jack Solomons did not in fact appear and Sam was rather disappointed not to come across any faces he recognised. He said it was preferable to meet agents or managers in likely places such as this rather than confront them across a desk in their office. This routine went on for several days without producing any results though my friend apparently made some tentative phone calls which I did not actually witness. After three days of this inactivity I was beginning to lose patience when Sam suddenly announced that he had arranged a meeting with the prestigious Foster's Agency which was just across the road from the hotel. He emphasised that he had made the appointment on my behalf and that I was on no account to divulge his name. What a surprise was in store for me!

We breakfasted at leisure and walked across a busy Piccadilly for our 10.00am rendezvous. Taking the lift to the first floor we were invited to take a seat until Mr Allen was ready to see us. In due course the telephone rang and we were ushered into Mr Allen's office, Sam thrusting me ahead of him having reminded me not to introduce him. For the moment he concealed himself behind me but as Mr Allen rose from his seat to greet me he caught sight of him and spluttered, 'Sam Rayne! We all thought you were dead!' It was without doubt a dramatic moment and I swear that Chesney Allen, (for it was indeed the legendary former partner of Bud Flanagan), turned a whiter shade of pale at this unforeseen confrontation. For Sam, I believe, it was a moment of triumph and justification. At last there was someone who testified to his rather celebrated past history.

Sam introduced me rather grandly as a young producer and impresario from Belfast, explaining our business, and Chesney Allen without further ado made some phone calls to sound out other agents and find out what artistes were free over the Christmas period. While still in the office the names Dennis Lotis and Edna Savage cropped up and we were given to understand that we were very lucky to find them available. I had heard of both of them and knew that Edna had been briefly married to the English rock and roll singer Terry Dene. I also recalled that Dennis Lotis had starred in the John Osborne musical, *The World of Paul Slickey*, which assured me that he had some acting experience. I had therefore no hesitation in giving my assent to whatever reasonable terms Mr Allen could arrange, merely pointing out that the Empire Theatre of Varieties was not a number one date and did not have the capacity of the larger Opera House. I left Sam to arrange the finer details as he and Chesney relived past memories of a world I knew little about and, in no time at all, a very fair deal was finalised, Fosters Agency taking no commission for their time or for the introductions to the other managers. During the general chatty conversation I happened to mention that I had tried to persuade Ruby Murray to take the role of Cinderella but that as early as the Blackpool summer season she had already been booked for Torquay. 'Funny you should mention that', said Chesney, 'but it has been said that Edna has modelled her style on Ruby's.' I began to feel that it was our lucky day.

An odd footnote to this extraordinary meeting occurred in the late 1970s when I was a host on the television chat show, *Afternoon Plus*. I had been interviewing the eccentric comedian Max Wall and afterwards he joined me for a drink after remarking that he had to kill a bit of time. Noting a twinkle in the ageing comic's eye, I very soon realised that he was giving himself a feed line for his next remark. 'Killing time!' he quipped. 'An odd occupation for a man of my age don't you think?' I hope I responded with a smile before enquiring if he had ever come across a comedian by the name of Sam Rayne. 'Did I know him?' he responded, 'I pinched his ending. Well we all thought he was dead and it seemed such a waste.' I never did find out what the ending was, but in his heyday he was obviously very highly thought of by his professional colleagues. It still seems sad to me that a sceptical Belfast doubted the word of a man who in his time was one of her famous sons.

Since it was just after 11.30am, Sam suggested we should book out of the Piccadilly Hotel and check in with Mama and Papa Olivelli in Store Street, off the Tottenham Court Road. It was where we had held the first night party for *Over The Bridge* but Sam had not been present

151

although I remembered he had recommended it as a favourite haunt of actors and variety artistes and also because of its proximity to the old Princes Theatre. It was yet another opportunity to take a trip down memory lane and I was sure Mama and Papa would welcome us with open arms. We were not disappointed. Sam, in particular virtually brought tears to Mama's eyes and of course the old couple remembered him in his prime which clearly delighted him. It was a fitting conclusion to our very successful mission and we returned to Belfast with almost all of my problems solved. For the moment the future looked bright, but what lay ahead I was yet to learn.

V

Back in Belfast, Peter Badger had been in charge and had directed the farce *Dry Rot* by John Chapman but now it was time to prepare for the pantomime. I of course told Henry about the encounter with Chesney Allen and he was very pleased with our choice of stars. One of the first problems that presented itself was how best to provide musical backing for Dennis Lotis in particular, when suddenly I thought of the guitarist Norman Watson, one of the finest all-round musicians in Belfast who could handle anything from classical guitar to jazz or flamenco and had brilliantly stood in at a moment's notice for Julian Bream as the soloist in the Rodrigues guitar concerto. It occurred to me that Norman with a small ensemble might appear onstage as the prince's personal musicians and with this thought in mind I rang our star's London agent. I was curtly dismissed with the brush off, 'Dennis Lotis is not Cliff Richard; he does not require any Shadows.' That comment seems particularly foolish after over half a century as Sir Cliff Richard continues to be one of the most durable stars of his generation; but my troubles were only just beginning.

Looking back on what I now realise was a 'crackpot' scheme to raise money for the production, an idea for which I take full responsibility, I cannot think what possessed me. Television advertising was then something of a novelty and some of the more visually creative scenarios, as well as catching the public's imagination, would fit rather aptly into our pantomime story. To take two examples which I remember clearly, one advert, promoting a new brand of cigarettes, portrayed a Sinatra-like figure pausing on a zebra crossing as a door was briefly opened by a glamorous girl and an orchestra played 'The Lonely Man' theme while a voice over intoned 'You're never alone with a Strand', would make a perfect first entrance for the prince, especially as the first number Dennis Lotis actually sang was *They're writing songs of love but not for me.* The second example concerned my then wife, Betty, who was playing 'The Fairy Snow'. Her first entrance was to occur as Buttons switched on a giant television set and she burst through the screen to a chorus of 'Hands that wash dishes can be soft as your face with new, new, Fairy Liquid.' Unfortunately neither Lever Brothers nor the tobacco company responded positively to our hair-brained request for sponsorship.

By contrast, local firms were keen supporters but I felt in all honesty I could not accept their financial backing because we were committed to going ahead with the other ideas without such support. Silver Cabs, a taxi firm, insisted on going ahead with the construction of a special car which entered, literally in a flash, when summoned by the prince's private detective as a mysterious voice intoned, 'Silver Cabs! There in a flash!' We refused their kind offer of money but the magic taxi was a huge success.

Rehearsals were about to begin when other snags arose. Sam Rayne had obviously lost his nerve and was not, therefore, prepared to make a come-back as the baron, who was now re-named 'the alderman'. Luckily John McBride made an excellent stand in. Then came a phone call explaining that one of the broker's men, (it was a double-act), was ill and would not be fit to travel. That is when someone, (I can't remember who), mentioned Frank Carson's name and at first sight I instinctively knew he was a larger than life performer; in fact he all but stole the show and we became lifelong friends. The next hurdle was handling the backing for the prince's songs. A preliminary band call left Dennis Lotis far from satisfied with the pit orchestra, and it was then that I mentioned the phone call to his agent and dropped the name of Norman Watson. Right away he responded positively and asked me to introduce him. I arranged an immediate meeting with Norman and we took a taxi to his house where we spent the entire night going through all the numbers in the script. Needless to say they got on famously and I was on the point of booking Norman and his ensemble, but there was one further snag. The Group by now had numerous engagements over the Christmas period. However, Norman had a pool of excellent musicians and thought he might be able to juggle the numbers and even provide a first-class stand-in for himself. This of course would not have been necessary if we had engaged him a few weeks earlier and Dennis was understandably annoyed with his agent for not consulting him. The Cliff Richard comparison was particularly irritating, I believe.

We began rehearsals in good heart and all went smoothly for a couple of weeks, though after looking at the advance bookings, I was by now pretty certain that takings at the box office were unlikely to match our production costs. At this time I was also suffering from exhaustion and decided to have a couple of day's rest, asking Paul Sharratt, who was an experienced pantomime performer, to become co-director of the show; Sam Rayne, who was nominally the producer, was, I could see, not up to the task and frankly, Dennis Lotis found him a bit of a pain. It was then I decided to share my worst fears with the Findlaters and a meeting of the directors was arranged which involved a day trip to Dublin. I travelled down with Frank, and Dermot Findlater, in the kindliest possible way, dropped the not entirely unforeseen bombshell. 'Jimmy', he said. 'as you already know, we have offered the theatre to the city of Belfast for the paltry sum of £30,000 and they have turned us down; but the estate agents, McKee and Company, who were handling that deal have come up with an offer just short of £90,000 from Littlewoods Stores who want to demolish the building in order to extend their premises in Ann Street. I'm afraid, to be fair to our shareholders, we have with great regret to accept that offer and so a theatre that has been in our family for generations will cease to exist.' Ironically, (and this has never been publicly disclosed), I was there to raise my hand in reluctant acquiescence to this shameful deal.

Meanwhile, unknown to me, Henry Lynch Robinson had attended an annual general meeting of CEMA, (later the Arts Council of Northern Ireland), and, supported by Alfred Arnold, had forcefully put the case for the public purchase of the Empire Theatre. Ironically it was the first AGM to be attended by my cousin, Kenneth Jamison, (later to become Director of the Arts Council of Northern Ireland), and so I was privileged to have a first-hand account of the proceedings. This account, in turn, I passed on to Maura Megahey who accurately records what happened in her book but I will briefly paraphrase it. The guest speaker was Sir Emrys William Williams, head of the Arts Council's London office. At an appropriate moment, Henry raised the question of the public purchase of the Empire Theatre which at the time was very much a 'live issue'. Pressing for a positive response he asked Sir Emrys what view the London office would have taken had an important 19th century theatre become available for purchase at an advantageous price. At this stage, sensing that Sir Emrys was under pressure, Mr Ritchie McKee as chairman felt obliged to intervene. 'There are serious structural faults', he blustered, 'I have had the theatre surveyed.' 'So have I', countered Henry who was a reputable architect, 'and in my considered opinion the faults are relatively minor and can be easily rectified without endangering the basic structure.' Resorting to invective, McKee described the theatre which as likely as not he had never set foot in, as 'nothing better than a flea pit.' So saying, this so-called lover of the theatre passed a death sentence on one of the architectural glories of Belfast and a repository of many of its most cherished memories though, to be honest, I doubt if it would have survived the dark years of 'The Troubles' when for so long the centre of Belfast was a 'No-Go' area.

Now of course the writing was on the wall and we had to face the inevitable. *The Evangelist* would not go on at The Empire and it would not be produced by Ulster Bridge Productions, though I believed then, and still believe, that Findlater & Company would have backed us if I had given the play the go-ahead. This was clearly not an option, for even if Sam had achieved the impossible and produced a workable script, there was not a chance of engaging at short notice a major star to play the eponymous role. It was the end of the line and my fellow directors reluctantly if inevitably had to agree, though Sam in his inimitable way could not resist remarking that in the end Ritchie McKee 'had got his revenge'.

There now remained the formality of the final rehearsals and staging of what was to be described as 'The Empire's last pantomime'. Perhaps, since it was a kind of epitaph, it is appropriate to recall its critical reception, citing Betty Lowry's review as a typical yardstick.

Taking cookery as her opening metaphor she begins her at times 'spinsterish' article with the following paragraph:

> "Take two pop singers, two comediennes, a group of Ulster straight actors; season with a sprinkling of English chorus girls partnered by young men of the type to be seen any night in a Belfast dance hall; flavour with a pinch of tradition and one of novelty. Mix well together. The result? A pantomime that has something for everyone but will satisfy no-one ..."

And ends it with:

> "It was a novel and ambitious project to set the pantomime in Belfast, to mingle tradition and modernity, straight actors and

variety artistes. It has not quite succeeded."

Much of her criticism was constructive and I think that I, for one, was working in a field of which I had little experience. She praised Dennis Lotis not only for his singing voice but also for his acting ability, which pleased me, but found little Edna Savage 'inaudible away from the microphone'. She also thought the talents of Elizabeth Begley and Kathleen Feenan were wasted in the slapstick roles of the ugly sisters and complained that neither of them had been given a funny line, all of which was fair comment; but most of the rest of the large cast which included Gerry Gibson, Frank Carson, Paul Sharratt, Betty Ellis, the Marie de Vere girls and their young male dancing partners, the Norman Watson Quartet, and others, were highly praised, so her summing up was perhaps a little one sided. She did not comment on the use of television commercials as part of the fun, nor did she pick out the leader of the young male dancers, whose name was Clarke, as a future jive world champion, who I had 'discovered' in the Plaza ballroom flinging the local girls around as if they were rag dolls. Other than these recollections only one vivid memory springs to mind. Calling me to his dressing room one evening after the performance, Dennis introduced me to an unassuming young man who, he said, had been a bus driver like himself. 'But', he said, 'he is on his way to becoming a very big star indeed.' It was Matt Monro.

The end of our story is all too predictable. Homeless, without resources and with no visible assets, we were forced into receivership; and so Ulster Bridge Productions, a company that had promised so much, ceased to exist early in the year 1961.

Of course it was a sad occasion and of course we had a meeting, albeit a brief and informal one, with each of us in turn trying to shoulder the blame, Henry for his apparent failure to deliver the goods with his pantomime, though I had overspent in the vain hope of sponsorship from companies we were advertising in our production, including Lever Brother's Fairy Liquid and the makers of Strand cigarettes. Sam apologised for his play not being ready, though I do not believe in retrospect he realised how high I was aiming in order to impress Laurence Olivier Productions. After our failure in London, it was my hope to show them that we had a play that could outdo *Over The Bridge*, and that it would appeal to a wider audience, especially with an American in the leading part.

Let me just say, that naturally, I, as artistic director of the company, took it upon myself to shoulder the major portion of the blame. Having helped Sam to make his work stage-worthy, I felt I should have run the last mile with him and put the second half of *The Evangelist* in order and on time; but then I am not a playwright and have never had any pretensions to be one. Nevertheless, the ending, after our spectacular success, was painful.

Postscript

There is little more to add, other than to relate the parting of the ways and its consequences. I bid farewell to Sam and Henry on the understanding that I was making an exploratory trip to London hoping to find work as a director but fully aware that I had more chance of landing the odd 'bit-part', likely as not as a southern Irish character with an assumed accent. Both Sam and Henry fully understood that I had a family to support and that I had literally no chance of finding employment here at home. As the poet Paul Yates was to put it many years later, I had 'offended' – against the establishment, that is – and for this reason was 'persona non grata'. It was not a comfortable feeling I may say, for someone who is a Belfast man through and through, and my sense of rejection was acute. Strangely enough I do not think this animosity involved Sam in quite the same way, despite the fact that he never missed an opportunity to attack the powers that be. His compelling play had, however, done the talking for him and he had the unswerving support of a working class community who at the time regarded him as their hero and spokesman. My crime had been to defy men who thought of themselves not only as my elders and betters but also as my employers and that, in their view, was unforgiveable.

My first place of lodging was a bedsit in Notting Hill gate where the bed folded back in a vertical position into the wall during the day, and where the only other amenities were an electric kettle and a gas ring with a frying pan and a couple of saucepans. My agent at that time was Roy Fox the former bandleader and I did not have to wait long for my first appointment which was at the fairly recently opened BBC Television Centre. To my surprise the interviewer was Ronald Mason, BBC Northern Ireland's radio producer for whom I had worked many times and who was to direct his first television play, which turned out to be Stewart Love's *The Randy Dandy*. When I arrived, I found Ronnie sitting behind a large desk flanked by two formidable gentlemen who turned out to be his English producers and he began by asking me rather hesitantly if I would consider playing one of the two speaking characters in the bookmaker's shop.

'But', I answered to their obvious surprise, 'there is no scene in a bookie's shop', quickly adding, 'and if there is, it's clearly a piece of padding, probably suggested, or even written by a scriptwriter.' To this day I don't know where I found the cheek, or the confidence, to meet this encounter head on; but I hadn't finished though I could plainly see that they were taken aback.

'Who is playing the part of the Randy Dandy?' I demanded.

'Well,' said one of the producers, 'the script is with Albert Finney at the moment.' I drew a deep breath.

'And what would Albert Finney know about playing a Belfast shipyard worker?' I asked. In the silence that followed I found myself rising to my feet. 'I'm sorry Ronnie', I said, 'I'm not interested in playing the man in the bookie's shop,' and with that I walked out of the office and along the corridor towards the lift. As the doors were opening I heard footsteps behind me and it was Ronnie.

'Would you consider reading for the part?' he asked me.

'Certainly, if they will give me a few minutes to familiarise myself with the bits they want me to read.' Back in the office the two producers explained apologetically that it was customary to book a star name for

162

their drama productions but since Ronald had spoken very highly of me they were prepared to give me a hearing. To cut a long story short, I was there and then given the leading role in the play and that audition turned out to be one of the most crucial encounters of my entire career. However, I was, I think, rather naïve to expect the absolutely ecstatic reviews it received in virtually every daily newspaper to produce immediate results. Stewart's play was never repeated, but I know for a fact that many people – particularly in the shipbuilding areas of Merseyside, Clydeside and Tyneside – remembered it for years afterwards. My second wife Robina, who I married in 1976, was amazed when I was recognised for my part as the Randy Dandy all those years later, rather than for my more prominent role in television. Once again I believe the unfamiliar Ulster accent was a stumbling block for producers and casting directors, and I waited in vain for the telephone to ring or for my agent to arrange further interviews. I had to wait until the latter half of 1961 for any significant developments, and ironically the first really positive move forward came in August when Granada Television were at last ready to screen *Over The Bridge* and I was offered the part of Archie Kerr, the Protestant bigot, rather than the mob leader, which at the time I thought was a mistake.

Meanwhile I had made the acquaintance of that wonderful actor Donal Donnely who became a really close friend and had invited me to take a share, amongst others, in a large basement flat at number 22 Ladbroke Crescent. 'You might as well', he joked, 'the half of Ireland stays here – you can represent the northern half!' Indeed it was a meeting place for actors from all parts of the Emerald Isle, some resident, some merely passing through or on speculative visits from Dublin and elsewhere, with all and sundry providing a pool of information as to what was going on in the worlds of stage, film and television in an unselfish way that rarely happens nowadays. It was there I got to know Godfrey Quigley, Norman Rodway, Milo O'Shea, Kate Binchey, Anna Managhan and many more, and we would often gather at Finch's pub in the Portobello Road before ending up at 'Number Twenty Two' as it was affectionately called. Also nearby, at Notting Hill Gate was the New Lindsay Theatre Club and it was there that I met Jack McGowran and renewed an old acquaintanceship in Pat Magee who were both appearing in *The Shadow of a Gunman*, a performance attended by its author Sean O'Casey and his lovely wife, Eileen. It was the only time I met the famous playwright, but many years later when I was re-introduced by his daughter Siobhán, Eileen O'Casey, still a lovely woman in her nineties, remembered me straight away and had my name and our meeting place on the tip of her tongue.

For the next few months we did what the majority of us did during the so-called 'resting periods' and signed on at the actor's labour exchange. At the time, Donal was courting his future wife Patsy Porter, a lovely girl who was principal dancer at Churchill's, the famous night club in Soho, patronised by world famous celebrities such as Frank Sinatra and Dean Martin. Donal would from time to time ask me to accompany him and we would sneak in with a flat half bottle of Irish whiskey concealed in one of our inside pockets. Donal knew the doormen and we would be nodded in to the glitzy interior where, having found a table near the stage, we would order a large bottle of ginger ale and two glasses. The trick was to add the whiskey when the waiter's back was turned and from our excellent viewpoint Donal could gaze adoringly at his beloved as she went through her excellently choreographed routines. In 2001, speaking from America, Donal appeared on my *This is Your Life* and I was very saddened to learn of his death in January 2010. He had a truly wonderful career and to have worked with him and shared a part of his life before he moved to America was a rare privilege.

One amusing episode occurred during the rehearsals for the televised version of *Over The Bridge* which took place in Putney, West London. I had told the director, John Moxey, that I thought Donal and I looked too alike to be playing the roles for which he had cast us; I the Protestant bigot and he the victimised Catholic worker and trade unionist. Since we were both living in the same flat I had shared this view with Donal and it was true that though we were different in stature we had frequently been mistaken for each other. Donal said he knew the rehearsal room and better still the pub next door which had a lovely landlady and would be an excellent place to have lunch. On the very first day we headed for the pub and the director accompanied us. As we reached the bar, Donal was about to introduce us when the landlady stopped him in his tracks with an exclamation of 'Don't tell me Donal, it's your brother!' I honestly believe that John Moxey thought he had been set up and he was certainly taken aback; it was nearly as good as a practical joke though it wasn't in fact 'a set-up'. I have actually seen a group photograph taken in BBC's Northern Ireland studios of the radio transmission of *Over The Bridge* with the actors grouped around the microphone listed as J.G. Devlin, James Ellis, Sam Thompson and Elizabeth Begley. In fact it was not me in the photo; it was my old friend Donal Donnely, so it would seem that circumstantial evidence bears witness to the resemblance.

The televised transmission of the play actually took place in one of Granada's old studios in Manchester and both it and the rehearsals brought back many happy memories. There were of course a number of cast changes including Donal who played Peter O'Boyle and the wonderful Finlay Currie who replaced an unwell Joseph Tomelty as Davy Mitchell. However, the television version, which was excellent, made up in a way for the failure of the stage version in London's West End and of course reached a nationwide audience.

Back at 'Number Twenty Two' the quest to establish ourselves on the first rungs of the thespian ladder was resumed, though Donal was already well on his way with an obviously shrewd agent who was proving to be a wise guide and mentor. It was now late October in 1961 and he had been considering a part in a new series for BBC Television to be called *Crime Patrol* but his agent had advised him to turn it down. Donal suggested that I contact his agent and get him to recommend me for the part. This I did and found myself being interviewed by David Rose. The series turned out not to be *Crime Patrol* but *Z-Cars* – it had been renamed – and the part I was being offered was that of a Liverpool Irish policeman called McGinty. There was no audition, with David simply asking me if I could do a Liverpool-Irish accent. Guessing that he probably didn't know what that was, and thinking on my feet, I launched into a dissertation on the subject beginning with 'But I am Liverpool-Irish', which I could see had won his undivided attention. I went on to explain that I had spent part of my childhood on Merseyside when my father had found work in Cammel Laird's shipyard in Birkenhead – 'The One-Eyed City' – and so I knew all the principal landmarks in Liverpool from the Pier Head and the docks to Lewis's large store, the Adelphi Hotel and Marks and Spencer's where my mother had bought my first suit for five shillings. Besides, I added, there were two kinds of Liverpool-Irish – those who had been there for generations and were indistinguishable from 'Scousers' and those who were starting a new life and still retained their Irish accents. I could sense that I had got the part and, emboldened, I hinted that the name McGinty was a just a bit 'Stage Irish'. David asked me to suggest another name which I did, and that was my contribution to the character that was to become PC Bert Lynch. The formalities over I was asked if I could catch a train to Liverpool that very evening and expenses and accommodation were quickly arranged as was a very favourable contract with my agent.

As I hurried back to 'Number Twenty Two' to pack a bag I told Donal it was not the same series that his agent had turned down, but when I arrived some hours later in Liverpool I was in for a big surprise. The wardrobe ladies were expecting me in a state of obvious panic and when one of them asked me to try on a uniform I was unable to get into it. Removing the trousers, I glanced at a name pad sewn inside the waistband which plainly said Mr Donal Donnely. Snatching it away in some embarrassment, the supervisor handed me another uniform which surprisingly fitted but in fact my agent had supplied the vital statistics. That evening I met my future colleagues who were Jeremy Kemp, Joseph Brady, Brian Blessed, Stratford Johns and Frank Windsor. The link with *The Randy Dandy* I was not to learn until much later. Two of the first six directors of *Z-Cars* who obviously had attended planning meetings to do with the crisis over Donal's withdrawal had either seen Stewart Love's play or, as in one instance, been involved in its production, and had put my name forward with strong recommendations. Such is the part that luck plays in all aspects of our unpredictable profession. However that may be, as the series was extended at first to thirteen episodes, then was prolonged indefinitely as it increased in popularity, I began to realise that my life had changed irrevocably and that my future career would by and large be based in England.

As ratings, recognition, critical response and the inevitable fan mail grew week by week for the entire team I began to realise that I had been cast in a television classic that was not only popular but of indisputable quality. What I did not foresee was that I would remain with it for over sixteen years and rise through the ranks from plain constable to Inspector Bert Lynch and would, as I later discovered, be responsible for many young men joining various police forces throughout the country. What really pleased me most, however, was the warm response in my native Belfast and I like to think that I have acted as a kind of ambassador for the people of Northern Ireland even in its darkest days during 'The Troubles'. Being the first North of Ireland voice to be heard regularly on national television and portraying, as Anne Devlin has said, 'a good policeman' has also I believe, paved the way for a younger generation of actors from my native province to make their mark across the water.

Though I have never once thought I needed to apologise for the stand taken on behalf of Sam Thompson and *Over The Bridge* I think I have more than compensated for any 'offence' against Northern Ireland's establishment. That stand, I am proud to say, and it has not gone unrecognised, ensured that never again would the authorities try to interfere in the affairs of the theatre, or attempt to unofficially censor the work of our local playwrights. Martin Lynch, who himself might be regarded in some quarters as controversial, recently revived *Over The Bridge* to mark the fiftieth anniversary of its first production. In his own sensitive and highly professional adaptation, and with a talented young director and strong cast, it played to packed houses and was even given financial support by the civic authorities. How times have changed! It is good to know that although it was nearly stillborn, Sam's 'masterpiece' has survived the test of time.

Needless to say, I was intensely curious at the time to hear news, if only at second hand, of the long delayed production of *The Evangelist*. Luckily Sam himself, accompanied by Jimmy Devlin, came to see me in London, and stayed in my flat in Holland Park where we chatted about old times. Sam told me that the production, staged at The Opera House, had been a success, if not quite on the scale of *Over The Bridge*. If my memory serves me right, I think his visit was sometime in 1964 and the BBC had postponed the transmission of Sam's third play, *Cemented With Love*, which had already been recorded. It was a curious decision in view of all that had happened but Jimmy told me he had assured Sam that it would be screened when they had got over their nerves.

I got the impression that though it was a friendly reunion and a fond memory, he was reluctant to share the trials and tribulations he had endured in order to mount *The Evangelist*, so I have relied on Maura Megahey's diligent research to put me in the picture. Apparently, though Louis Elliman, the proprietor of Dublin's Gaiety Theatre, was prepared to go ahead with the project, director after director seemed to find flaws and difficulties with *The Evangelist*. Denis Carey, who was artistic director of the Bristol Old Vic company when I was a student there, was otherwise engaged. Harold Goldblatt, as ever cautious, advised Sam not to publicise his involvement and said that no progress could be made until there was a final script and suggested that the play would 'benefit from a different ending'. Tyrone Guthrie's opinion was that although there were marvellous things in the play, he added ominously that 'it bristles with monster headaches for the director'. He also commented that the play was in a very rough state and that, if Sam were interested, Guthrie might make his own changes. It would appear that Sam, probably in desperation, 'edited' the great man's comments by telling a reporter that Guthrie was interested in his play and thought that it only needed 'minor changes'. Even Hilton Edwards, who finally directed the play, observed that the writing was 'careless, as if set down hurriedly … with racing pulses and warm blood.' As I have said earlier, I can see little material difference between the published version of the play, (apart, that is, from the choice and placement of some of the hymns), and the manuscript copy of the play which I still have in my possession.

Although I was totally unaware of it at the time, Cecil Tennant, the theatrical agent and manager of Laurence Olivier, intended to have *The Evangelist* produced in London, which had been my burning ambition back in 1960. Apparently Tennant was searching, even after Sam's death, for a collaborator or co-author to make the play a plausible commercial proposition for the West End stage. Unfortunately this project did not materialise, though naturally I find it a tantalising idea to speculate on the impossible dream. Would he, I wonder, have considered the possibility, as I did, of persuading Olivier to play the leading role? After all, he had by then starred in John Osborne's *The Entertainer* and was on the lookout for contemporary plays, but it would have been the ultimate irony I feel, had Sam not lived to see his final triumph. The fact remains, however, that he is above all remembered, and remembered fondly, for his triumph over censorship,

169

and though I still maintain, now more than ever after reading Dr Megahey's absorbing book, that *The Evangelist* was, to use my own words, 'never finished' and that his best play and ultimate masterpiece was in the final analysis, *Over The Bridge*.

In the intervening years I had often thought of those heady days in 1959: the congenial times spent with Sam, the journeys between Belfast, Dublin and London, and my eventual departure from the land of my birth. Those thoughts led me to write this poem, named after Sam's greatest play.

OVER THE BRIDGE

I crossed the Bridge and thought to shake the dust
From off my feet, but it was not to be;
For though I fled across the Irish Sea,
Nursing resentment and profound disgust

That individuals had betrayed their trust
And held the public stage in ignominy,
 Events o'ertook the ancient enemy,
And time has mellowed memory, as it must.

Homeward I crawl, a wretched prodigal,
To bide awhile, and then again depart–
To leave once more, once more to feel bereft–

Your picture album in my mental holdall,
The hills of Antrim etched upon my heart,
For, truth to tell, I never really left.

Acknowledgements

This book is a first-hand account, largely from memory, though prompted and refreshed by assisting Maura Megahy during a part of her research for her splendid book, *The Reality of his Fictions: The Dramatic Achievement of Sam Thompson*, published by Lagan Press in 2009. To her I am eternally grateful for without her untiring efforts and reciprocal exchanges of hard facts and verifiable evidence, I very much doubt if this book would have materialised.

Press reports, though not infallible (and those I considered unreliable I have corrected or simply ignored), were by and large accurate and to the newspapers of the time, particularly the *Belfast Telegraph*, I am likewise grateful for keeping a controversial issue alive over a period of nine months or more.

Some 'authorities' I have tended to overlook on the grounds that they were conjectural and therefore uninformed. Both at the time and subsequently, it has seemed to me that everyone, from the man in the street to theatre historians, poets, play producers and academics have wanted to air their views or be seen to be a part of the action and as often as not have simply been wide of the mark. The notable exception in my opinion is Dr Maura Megahey.

Of course my cousin, Dr Kenneth Jamison OBE, was very much a part of the scene before his appointment as Director of the Arts Council of Northern Ireland. In fact he designed and painted the front gauze for *Over The Bridge* (one of the few visual images which has survived the passing of years) as well as designing the set for Joseph Tomelty's *A Shilling for the Evil Day* and making a model for *The Evangelist* which was never staged by Ulster Bridge Productions. He and I have often 're-lived' those heady days and our talks and discussions, as well as his availability to check certain developments in which he was involved have been both a stimulus and inspiration.

One error, albeit not a major one, although it is apparently recorded in Sam Hanna Bell's journal, is that the after the performance party on the opening night of *Over The Bridge* was held at the home, (flat), of the painter George McCann and his wife Mercy, where the poet Louis McNiece was staying, and attended by, among others Sam Hanna Bell himself, Henry Lynch Robinson and the author and his wife – i.e. Sam and May Thompson. My cousin recalls that he had dinner at the McCann's, before the performance, and it is unthinkable that Sam would have deserted his colleagues and fellow actors on this particular occasion. I have no doubt whatsoever that this did not occur because the party, which involved a huge cast and their guests, the directors of the Empire Theatre with their friends and the triumphant playwright himself, with his wife, celebrated until the early hours. Unfortunately this 'error' found its way into Maura's book through no fault of her own.

Other names to whom I am indebted include another very old friend from schooldays, the actor James Greene who, with Kenneth Jamison, read an early draft of the book, the latter virtually proof reading, making many constructive suggestions and alterations, and offering unfailing encouragement. Nearer home, in our village in Lincolnshire, I am grateful to Alex Royall who sorted out, for me, insoluble computer problems.

My thanks also to Brian Garrett who, goes back a long way in this story, and has acted as Sam's literary representative during his lifetime and been his executor since his death. He has protected his reputation, looked after the interests of his widow May, who has sadly since died, and his son Warren; and most recently smoothed the way for Martin Lynch's excellent adaptation of *Over The Bridge* which I feel certain will keep the play alive for the present generation of playgoers. I have already referred to the poet Tom Paulin in the foreword and his recently found postcard, of November, 1992, may well have been the spur for this rather belated endeavour.

Thanks

This book was made possible with the help of the family of Lord (Billy) Blease, David Chick, Mr & Mrs A. Dunn, Bernard Fitzpatrick BL, Jim Fitzpatrick, Brian Garrett, Erskine Holmes, Patrick Keane FRCS, John A.D. Kennedy, David Kenning, Michael Lavery QC, Cecilia Linehan, Boyd Logan, W. James Maginnis, Stratton Mills, Frank McCartan, Professor Garth McClure, Stephen Prenter FCA, Damian Smyth, Mr & Mrs Justin Terry, Denis Tuohy and Robin Walsh.